Bruce Gordon,
14, Glebe Terrace,
Helmsdale,
Sutherland.

GEORDIE

GEORDIE

By

DAVID WALKER

COLLINS
ST JAMES'S PLACE, LONDON

FIRST IMPRESSION	JULY, 1950
SECOND IMPRESSION	AUGUST, 1950
THIRD IMPRESSION	SEPTEMBER, 1950
FOURTH IMPRESSION	OCTOBER, 1950
FIFTH IMPRESSION	NOVEMBER, 1950

PRINTED IN GREAT BRITAIN
COLLINS CLEAR-TYPE PRESS : LONDON AND GLASGOW

To

HULDAH   RENNIE

* I *

IT was half-past eight of a Saturday morning. Geordie took the path which ran round behind the Bighoose. He was wearing his tackety boots, but the path was mossy so the nails didn't make hardly any noise as he flitted along between the trees like a Red Indian. Perhaps not a Red Indian; fourteen past was too old an age for to be playing wee boy's games, but stalking was good practice; you never knew when you mightn't get into some adventure where a man needed to move as quiet and stealthy as a hunting cat.

He saw Jean from a good way off. She was sitting on the dry stone dyke looking across the way to where the big loch was shimmering in the sun and a boatload of fishers was out to an early start. Geordie slipped like a shadow from tree to tree. He'd be right up close to her in a minute and she hadn't spotted him.

" Hallo, wee Geordie," she said, not turning her head.

" Hallo, wee Jean," said Geordie. He was just a bit vexed, but he hid it that way.

" I'm bigger'n you."

Geordie let that go by. It was true she was taller, and her only thirteen.

" Did ye bring a sangwich-piece? "

" Ay," said Jean. " Mine's cheese. What's yours? "

" Mine's pork," said Geordie. " Come away then! "

Geordie climbed over the dyke and they set off along the path beside the burn. It was warm for May, not a breath of wind, and the mist still hanging on the high tops.

" Did you tell yer dad where we was going? "

Geordie shook his head. " I never said. Dad's away on the bus for to get snare-wire. He didn't ask, so I never said nothing."

" You're a canny wee crater, but you'll maybe get a licking for it yet."

" Don't call me wee," said Geordie. Twice was too much.

" Och sorry, Geordie." Jean was only a lassie, and a bit cheeky, but she was as good as another boy to be with. She'd think things out twice as quick as Geordie would. So he was slower and smaller than she was, but him being a year older that made them equal. They were good pals, growing up together in a place where folk were scarce.

They walked fast up the path between the stunted birch trees and out on to the open moor. It was a rare morning right enough, with the beads of dew on the cobwebs on the heather. Cock grouse were calling all round. They were tame like always in the nesting season, half dopey, hardly paying heed to Geordie and Jean. "Go-back, Go-back," they called, and the wattles were swollen and red above their eyes.

But Geordie and Jean did not heed them either. They were going to the eagles' nest at the head of the glen. Geordie's dad got paid for rearing the eagles safe, which was why Geordie hadn't told him.

"Will they be hatched yet, Geordie?"

"I dinna' ken. It takes an awful long time for eagles to hatch."

They walked for another hour before they saw one of the golden eagles soaring high over the hill. It was still far away, but even at that distance the bird looked big. It wheeled alone in the sky.

"Could be a buzzard," said Jean doubtfully.

"No, it couldn't," said Geordie. "The eagle wouldn't let a wee buzzard fly over its nest. Would you if you was an eagle?"

Jean was silent, not challenging Geordie on his own ground, for Geordie's dad was keeper and stalker, and Jean's dad was gardener. Just the same way, Geordie couldn't have a right knowledge of flowers and growing things, not like the knowledge Jean had inherited from her dad.

The burn was much smaller now. It wound up the glen in front of them, and the noise of the tumbling water was always in their ears. It was brown clear water, playing over and round the grey stones and between the peaty banks; peaceful to-day, but it could be fierce when it carried the torrents of a thunder-plout. Then you wouldn't know it for the same wee burn.

They passed the hill bothy, a grey stone hut with a stall where the pony could wait for its load home in the stalking season. Beyond the hut the hills closed in tight around them. The heathery moor was away behind now, and even in the warm sunshine of May the hillsides were cold and grey, grey lichen on grey rocks.

Geordie had been up many times with his dad but he still felt a lonely feeling there. It wasn't a thing you would talk about; you would just feel it round about you and in behind the back of your neck, and you would like it too.

" It's a kind of a skeery place," said Jean in a

small voice. Being a lassie she could say what a boy wouldn't want to be saying.

" It's just what you're used to," Geordie said, meaning he was used to it and she wasn't.

And then they reached the very head of the glen where the sun didn't shine. The eagle swung out of sight above the hill.

" There's the nest," said Geordie, pointing up the hill face in front of them. There was a steep bed of scree and above that a broken cliff. The eyrie was on a ledge up there. They could see part of the tangled pile of sticks, but there was no sign of either of the eagles.

" We'll sit," Geordie stated. So they sat down against a rock and waited for developments. They sat for a long time and nothing happened and the warmness died out of them. Jean gave a shiver. She had on her old kilt and a jersey, and she had thin bare legs. She looked hardy, more like a boy than a girl except for the long pigtails and the softer face she had. But there was nothing soft about her. Geordie was wearing the shorts made out of dad's old tweed, and he was beginning to feel cold too, even through his jersey.

The eagle came very fast. He just came from nowhere, and they both saw him swoop low across the rocks with a blue hare as large as life in his claws; and he spread all the feathers of his wings against the air so they stood out like broad fingers, and he landed at the nest.

" The eggs must be hatched," said Geordie. He stood up. There wasn't any use sitting there getting chilled now that the bird had come.

Then the eagle flew again and his mate too, and they both flew round above the nest, showing first against the rock and then against the sky, calling all the time. It was like a whistle the noise they made, and they were in a rare state of excitement.

" Come on," said Geordie. " We'll just take a wee peek and come away."

So he began to climb up the loose slithery scree with Jean struggling along behind him. The two eagles went on swinging above them. They looked terrible big and dark and fierce, but Geordie was going to see the young ones in the nest. That was what he'd come for, and even an eagle has a worse bark than a bite, or that was what dad said. Dad said a missel-thrush was fiercer at the nest than an eagle. Still, Geordie couldn't help knowing that a missel-thrush didn't have beak and claws strong enough to tear the head off you. But he went on. Dad said, " Even if you're a wee snippet of a laddie, Geordie, I'll grant you have the detairmination."

Soon he reached the top of the scree, and he

stopped a minute to see what was the best way to go. The nest wasn't far above, thirty feet perhaps and most of that was broken rock. There was just the last bit below the ledge that looked more difficult.

One of the eagles dived down so it passed below Geordie. It wasn't close, but he could hear the swish of the wings and he could see that fierce head turned to watch him all the way. Geordie waved his stick at it.

Now he was right in below the ledge and Jean was still close behind him. He could hear the young ones mewing and thrashing about up there at their dinner. The big eagles were stooping closer.

This was the difficult bit, but Geordie could see the way well enough. There was just the one way. You had to shuffle along a narrow ledge to the left for ten feet with your hands on the ledge above, where the nest was. Then when you got farther along, the two ledges came closer together and you could get back to the nest along the top. There was a bit of a drop below, but it was easy enough if the eagles didn't take a dab at you, and if you were tall enough to reach that ledge.

" Watch out, Geordie! " said Jean with a squeak in her voice.

He swung his stick again. This time the eagle

was close, and the wind of its passing was a very loud noise. Geordie tied his hankie on to the stick and gave it to Jean. " You wave that, Jean," he said.

He wormed his way on to the narrow ledge and stood there, reaching up with his hands; but he couldn't reach the ledge above. All the rest of the rock-face was bare, no hand holds. Geordie tried again, standing on the very tips of his toes, straining his hands up till he was near busted. But he couldn't do it. He just couldn't reach, and he knew very well that there was no way he could get up to the eagle's nest. It was an awful bad feeling with him having the idea in his head all these weeks.

He sat down again beside Jean.

" I'm going, Geordie," said Jean. She had her mouth tight closed and she was a wee thing pale, but he knew from her face that she was decided to go up to the nest.

He said nothing; just took the stick from her.

Jean stood up. Her tackety boots scuffled on the rock. She reached up far. Then she had her fingers on the ledge and she began to go along sideways, taking it slow. There she was with her droopy tattered kilt and her thin lassie's body. She's a braw lassie, Geordie, thought, and he felt downhearted that it was her and not him, but proud of her too.

He kept swinging the stick with the hankie on it. The eagles were in a rare state, diving and squealing close by and going round and round like a circus, and Geordie had to shout to keep them off. His voice echoed from across the hill, and again and again, fading, sounding from all round the closed place.

Jean had reached the other end and was coming back along the top ledge now. " There's twa great muckle chicks wi' feathers on them, Geordie."

" Come away back, Jean," he called.

She hesitated at the far end again, looking down at the drop below, and then over her shoulder at the angry birds in the sky.

" Keep your eyes on the rock! " said Geordie sharply. It wouldn't do for her to get scared now.

Then she slipped along the ledge and back beside him. They went downhill, over the broken rocks, over the rattling scree, into the wet shadows where the sun didn't reach, and on till they came to the murmuring start of the burn. They sat down in the sunlight and took out their sangwich-pieces and divided them up so that they each had half of cheese and half of pork, and no word spoken yet. The eagles were soaring high again above the hill.

Geordie looked at Jean. " You're braw," he said. It was the highest praise he had inside him and he had to give it to her, even although he felt terrible that a lassie could do what he hadn't been able to do. He ate the pork one first.

Jean blushed scarlet. " So're you, Geordie," she said. She ate the cheese first.

But even if it was Jean who had done it, and even if Georgie knew she wouldn't go telling folks, he couldn't get over the sick feeling that she was a year younger and he was too wee. It stayed with him all the way down, so they walked without speaking, and he hardly noticed the grouse and the blue hares and the whaup crying beside the bog and the mother mallard taking her young ones for a swim in the hill loch. Geordie was fed up at himself. Here he would be leaving the school soon, and no bigger than a bantam in among the cockerels and pullets.

They stopped where the paths separated.

Jean stood there. " Thanks, Geordie," she said. She looked kind of shy and there was trouble in her grey eyes. She was an awful good pal to him. She turned to go and then turned back. " Every-

body can't be big, Geordie," she said, and went off
down the hill.

When Geordie got home he could hear his mum
moving about in the house. He went round to the
woodshed for some logs. That was one of his jobs,
keeping mum in sticks for the fire. He took one
load and went back for another.

She was in the kitchen the second time he stag-
gered in with an armful.

" Ye're a guid wee soul, Geordie," she said,
standing at the range with her back to him.

✶ 2 ✶

GEORDIE went straight out of the kitchen and up the rickety steps to his own room. It was small, in below the roof of the cottage, and there was just space for his bed and the dresser with his hairbrush on it. He took a look at himself in the mirror. Somehow you'd expect when you felt so bad that it would show in your face; but there was no difference. It was the same awful red face and the same carroty hair. That was wee Geordie in the mirror, wee to Jean, wee to the boys at the school, wee to dad and mum. Too wee to be any use for anything, too wee to be as good as a lassie in a climb.

There were some old magazines in the corner of the room. Geordie had read them all before, for he was a great reader even if reading took time because he was slow in his thoughts as well as in his growing. But he needed something to do to take his mind off his troubles, so he fetched a couple of mags and took off his boots for fear mum would come up and catch him with them on the bed and he lay on his back and began to read the old stuff again. There were some adventure stories and some about love. He never bothered with the love ones. Love was daft. But he liked fine to read adventure.

His favourite was about a boy asleep in bed at night and he wakes up sudden and hears noises in the house, so he ups and tiptoes to the door not making any creak on the boards. " Please turn to page 46," it said when the story was just getting exciting. Geordie knew fine what was coming, but it still had him gripped every time he read it, so he flipped over fast to page 46 hardly able to wait for the boy to crack the burglar over the head and be the hero of the village.

Here was page 46 and . . . But Geordie stopped. He was seeing something he'd never noticed any of the other times. It stood up on the printed page and smacked him in the eye. He looked away to go on reading the story, and looked back again. That was how it smacked him, and him being the boy in the dark house not knowing what was round the corner, and then forgetting all that quite sudden.

It was an advertisement, tucked up there in the corner, an advert with two small pictures. Geordie read it through once. Then he read it again. This is what he read:

" ARE YOU UNDERSIZED? DO PEOPLE IGNORE YOU? NO NEED FOR DESPAIR! GROW BIG THE SAMSON WAY! WRITE FOR MY ONLY UNIQUE COURSE IN PHYSICAL CULTURE. YOU CAN BE STRONG! YOU CAN BE TALL! BALANCED DEVELOPMENT IS MY MOTTO. WORLD-WIDE TESTIMONIALS. FOR PROOF OF SUCCESS SEE UNTOUCHED PHOTOGRAPHS BELOW.

SEND TEN SHILLINGS ONLY FOR COMPLETE COURSE IN PLAIN WRAPPER. YOUR PROBLEMS WILL RECEIVE PERSONAL ATTENTION OF THE GREAT HENRY SAMSON, SIX FOOT FOUR AND THE WORLD'S STRONGEST MAN.

WRITE P.O. BOX 689, WADSWORTH, LONDON, N.10. SATISFACTION GUARANTEED."

Geordie suddenly felt very tired. He didn't know why that should happen to him; a ten-mile walk up the glen was nothing on a Saturday; nothing ever made him tired, even if he was small. Perhaps it was just the great idea striking him. Yes, it must be that. He closed his eyes for a minute, lying quite slack, seeing wonderful pictures of him big and strong. Then he opened his eyes again to read the advert. The man was a wee stoopy thing BEFORE, but he had a chest like a barrel on him AFTER, and tall.

Ten bob was a big price. It was a huge price; and how would you know it wasn't just a have-on? Them English with their fancy ways. What dad said came into his mind—"it's jest blether blether wi' the Sassenachs, full o' fancy capers. I've no time for them."

But he looked again. There was something about it that wasn't just English Blether: " World-wide testimonials, before and after, six foot four, satisfaction guaranteed."

No, it read like it was true. Ten bob was a lot, but he'd earned more than that at the potato-picking last year. Still, that was last year and he didn't have ten bob now.

Geordie went over to the dresser and took his money-box out of the drawer. He undid the sticky tape and opened the box, knowing near enough what was there, but not knowing exactly. He counted it up. Seven shillings and eightpence it came to. The eightpence would do the postal order and the stamp. That left three bob to get.

Generally Geordie took a long time to decide things; but not now. He'd made up his mind already what he was to do, and he knew that the Samson course, English or no, was a right good bargain. He was sure of it. What was ten bob if you could be as big as Henry Samson?

But first get the money. There was no work for boys in May. Well, mum was the only hope.

He put on his boots and went down to the kitchen. Mum was washing up the dishes over at the sink. He stood in the doorway looking at her broad back. She didn't pay any attention. Maybe she hadn't heard him for the clatter of bowls and plates.

" Mum! " he said.

" What is it, Geordie? " said mum, going on with what she was doing.

" Mum, could you loan me three bob? I need it special."

She stopped then, and gave her hands a wipe on the towel, and turned round.

" Three bob," she repeated, looking at him half serious, but gentle, like she always was. " That's a lot, Geordie. What's it for ? "

He wasn't going to tell her what for. He'd decided that quick, like everything else about the Samson course. He wasn't going to tell anybody.

" I'll pay back after the tattie-picking," he said. " It's special."

" What for, though, Geordie? "

" I'm not saying." Geordie hung his head. " Och, come on, Mum! '

She laughed and went over to the cupboard. He knew he was going to get it. " You and yer secrets, Geordie. It's just a loan, mind. There you are, my wee laddie." She gave him the three bob.

" Thanks, Mum," he said, and popped right upstairs again. Her calling him wee every minute of the day, and everybody else too. Well, he wasn't caring, not now he had the money for the course. There were going to be surprises for folks one of these days when they found wee Geordie was as big as Henry Samson. Geordie didn't feel tired any more.

Now he had to write the letter. It wasn't the spelling that Geordie was worried about. Teacher said he wasn't a bad speller. No, it was sending all that money in a P.O. away down to England when you couldn't know what tricks they mightn't be up to before the letter ever got to Henry Samson. And then it was important to make sure of getting Henry Samson's personal attention. It said you would, but you couldn't be certain, not with all the clerks and typists there might be.

Geordie got some paper and practised at the letter. It took him a lot of practice so it was near tea-time when he had it right in the end and could copy it out fair.

He put the address at the top. Then he wrote:

" Dear Sir (Mister Henry Samson)

Please send by return complete course to yours trooly in plain wrapper. I am fourteen past and wee for my age, so I need hight and strenth. Here is ten shillings in a P.O.

Hoping this finds you as it leaves me, in the pink.

Geordie Mactaggart "

Geordie wrote the envelope too. He put it all away for Monday morning when he'd go to the post office before school. Then he went down for his tea.

Well, no sooner was it away on Monday forenoon than Geordie began to wonder when he'd be hearing. Two days down and two days back was what he expected, although there wasn't much to go on, him never having done no writing that you'd notice down to England and back. So every day when he came back from the school he'd look in the kitchen and then up in his room in case mum could have put it there.

But it was Saturday morning when the letter came, and that was lucky for Geordie because he didn't go to school on Saturdays, and he hung about and caught postie at eleven o'clock and took the plain brown envelope. There wasn't any post for dad and mum, just for Geordie. " Mr. G. Mac-Taggart," it said on the envelope. He stuffed it in his trouser pocket and went away up the hill to find a place where he could read about the course without disturbance.

That was a morning Geordie never forgot, not in all his life. It had been cloudy weather all week, but it was fine again to-day and there were white fluffy clouds hurrying across the sky. You could see spring in the pale young leaves and smell it in the flowers and hear it in the honey bees humming by and in the low bumble of the fat bumbles.

Geordie went as far as the old granite quarry which was half a mile from home. It was a deserted place. Nobody went there except dad whiles to ferret the rabbit burrows, but he wouldn't be doing that in the month of May.

He sat down on a big rock where it was shady and opened the brown envelope. It was a wee bit of a disappointment just to find paper inside. That was all you would expect, but after paying the ten bob and all the rest of it, somehow you thought there might be something more mysterious than a thin bundle of papers.

The letter was from Henry Samson himself, and the heading stamped on it was:

Henry Samson
Physical Culture Expert and World's Champion

Then it said, all typed out lovely:

" DEAR GEORDIE,

Thanks for yours of 20th inst. and 10/- P.O. I take pleasure in welcoming you as a student and enclose the Course herewith. Now remember, eat plenty, keep on at your exercises, and say the Henry Samson Success Poem ten times every day. If at first you don't succeed, try try try again. Keep trying, that's what I mean. I'm sending you the secrets but it's up to you to carry them out and nothing but hard work can bring success. I am taking a personal interest in your case, Geordie, so keep me posted how you get on. Here is my photo as a special gift and for an inspiration.

Yours truly,

HENRY SAMSON "

Well, that was a lovely letter. It made you feel Henry Samson was near beside you taking a special interest. And the photo, all signed and everything. Geordie had never seen such a huge man as Henry

Samson looked. He was wearing a pair of tiger-skin drawers, and his muscles bulged out every which way. He was great.

Geordie got settled down to reading about the course, about the stretching exercises and the developing exercises, all about everything. And he learned the Success Poem. It was a fine one, a real good poem. It said:

> " To-day I may be small
> But soon I shall be tall,
> I'll be strong
> I'll be long
> I'll grow the Henry Samson way,
> Gaining a fraction every day.
> Sound as a bell
> Feeling my muscles swell
> *I'm the good old English bull-dog breed,*
> *And Samson will teach me to succeed.*
> (last two lines to be repeated) "

Geordie changed one word in the poem. Then he had it for his very own. He was just practising the first stretching exercise which needed you to lie down flat on the ground, hands behind your head, and raise your middle off the ground as high as you could ten times, and it was hard work after two or three, when he heard dad's voice calling from above him.

" What's up, Geordie? " said dad.

Geordie scrambled to his feet. He picked up the letter and the photo and the wee course book, and he was fair mad at being caught by dad and he didn't know what to say.

Dad was standing at the edge of the quarry looking down. He had Bess, the Labrador, with him and she had a worried expression too.

" Och, I was jest practisin', Dad," said Geordie, feeling very small indeed down there.

" Come away then," said dad. " It's past dinner time."

So they walked down together, and dad didn't say any more about Geordie's strange antics. He'd been up to the big plantation after hoody crows, and he told Geordie about that, and then they were back home, and Geordie thought, well, perhaps dad didn't notice anything funny.

He got started on his course by eating a right big dinner. Now that he knew Henry Samson took a special interest in him he was going to put his whole heart into it from start to finish, and Geordie had a big heart.

But dad had noticed all right. Geordie was

outside the window after dinner and he heard dad say to mum:

" You ken the old quarry."

" Ay."

" I came by there, and Geordie was lyin' stretchit and grunting something awful. Practisin' he said he was, but it looked gey queer to me. Is the wee laddie all richt? "

" Och, he's fine," said mum. " He ate a rare big dinner. Was it mebbe exercises he was doing? "

" Could be," said dad. " He was dour-like, so I didn't ask much. Ye ken the way he is? "

Mum laughed. " Ay, I ken," she said. " He's up to something, is our Geordie, but I'm thinking it's just mebbe exercises to make him grow. That's what it could be."

Mum was awful fly, much flier than dad.

* 3 *

IT was just like what Mister Samson meant when he said, keep trying. It was a slow business, and there were whiles when Geordie felt hudden-doon, and thought he would never succeed. But he stuck it out like a real MacTaggart, and in the end the results began to come. Six months passed and Geordie had stretched two inches; a year went by and he was still longer and broader and he looked down an inch into Jean's grey eyes. He was finished with the school that summer, and he went to work with dad learning the keeper's job. First thing in the morning before work he would do the stretching exercises, winter or summer, dark or light, and the floors of the old stone cottage would tremble with Geordie's exertions, and dad and mum grumbled at first. But they got used to the shaking; it was like living near a railway line and being accustomed to the dancing of the pots and pans. And last thing at night Geordie did the strengtheners; and in between, any time when he had a spare minute, he would lie and stretch in the snow, or throw rocks for strength across the whispering burns in summer.

He ate huge meals too, near half a gallon of porridge and milk and salt and no sugar every morning standing up beside the kitchen table, and mum would say, " That's a terrible capacity you've got, Geordie." But the porridge was just a beginning to the day. There would be stew and spuds and oatcakes and good butter and milk from Jessie the cow, and the bigger Geordie got the more pleased mum and dad became. They loved Geordie big or small, but they liked fine to have a muckle laddie for a son.

Everyone was pleased except Jean. That was a queer thing, her liking him when he was wee, and then treating him rude as soon as he began to build up. She was more like a stranger at times, and other times she'd just laugh at him. It was worrying for Geordie. She had a sharp tongue that could make him feel wee-er than he had ever felt when he was wee.

" Hallo, Tarzan," she said one day when she caught him having a short in-between practice in the wood near the Bighoose. " How's the muscles?"

" Fine, Jean," he said sheepishly.

" You'll be an elephant afore ye're through."

She said it nastily, as nastily as a lassie like Jean could say anything, for she was growing bonny and was kind to all the world but Geordie.

He didn't speak.

" I mean it," she said.   " You're daft.   It's a fixed idea, and you're just making yourself into a muckle stupid lump."

" Och, Jean," said Geordie.   He didn't understand why she aye had to be after him.   He had his mind made up, and he wasn't going to change, not even for Jean.

" Dinna' och at me," she said, and tossed her dark head that wasn't in pigtails any more, and went away off through the wood.

Now the autumn when Geordie was sixteen came round, and the winds were strong and it was the back of the year when the hind shooting was half-way through.   Geordie and his dad had been on the hill all day.   They had got one hind in the morning early and had walked a long way after that.   But the weather had turned bad, rain and sleet off and on, and that started the deer moving about the open hill, seeking shelter, and they were skeery, trotting a mile and standing nervously, changing direction with the wind, giving no chance to the man and the boy. In the end dad led wide round a big shoulder.

" I believe that's the way they're going," he said, " but I can't be sure. The beasts are daft the day. If we don't get into them this time, we'll go home. You can take the shot, Geordie."

So dad and Geordie took a last wide sweep below the wind. The hill was dark, cold in colour and in air, and grey cloud misted all the tops. Their boots brushed against the tough heather roots and squelched into the black soil below. It was a bad afternoon, but a day when a man who knew the hill could love its bleakness. That was the way a man would keep it in his mind.

Dad stopped below the crest. He went up slowly on hands and knees and looked between the heather clumps. His bright-checked tweed mixed in with the green and black and grey and brown of the moor, so you would hardly notice him from ten yards off. He slid back again.

" It's a small lot," he whispered. " Take the old one, Geordie. But go canny! They're skeery."

Geordie had the rifle out of its cover. He crawled up the way dad had gone, first on hands and knees, then out flat, sliding along with his elbows and toes. He raised his head slowly when

c

he came to the place. They weren't more than a
hundred yards away, every head up. They were
suspicious, but they hadn't seen him. The old
hind was on the right. He sank down again and
rested with his face in the wet heather till he got
his breath; a belly crawl took the puff out of you
quicker than anything.

Then he was ready. He slipped over the safety
catch, rose on his elbows and took slow aim just
behind the old one's dark shoulder. Hold your
breath, squeeze don't pull, all the things dad had
taught him.

The noise of the shot cracked in his head and
rang away all round the moor and he reloaded
quickly. The old hind flopped on her face, no
need of a second shot at her and no chance of one
at the others. They were off at full gallop, hooves
scampering hollow, then out of earshot, pale scuts
bobbing, swiftly over the next rise and out of
sight.

Geordie and dad walked forward over the boggy
ground. The hind was still alive. She lay low in
front, paddling a little with her hind legs, straining
her long-eared head.

" A bad shot," said dad severely. The bullet
had gone in just above the heart. Geordie stood
there a moment. " Get on with it, laddie! " What

you started you finished, that was dad's rule with Geordie.

He took out his knife and gripped the hind by one of her long ears. You couldn't help seeing the look in the eyes when you did that. She gave her last and only bark out of the bottom of her throat. Then the knife was in, and the dark blood gushed out.

Dad watched till Geordie had finished the gralloch. "It's too soft here for the pony," he said. "We'll need to drag her."

So they each took a leg and pulled the dead beast out of the hollow and over the rise and all the way across the big bog where the treacherous places were the brightest green. It was hard hauling when they went down over their knees. Geordie noticed suddenly that dad was flagging. That was a surprise; and he saw that his face was pale, not red like it usually was.

" Let me take it, Dad," he said. Geordie was well able, five foot ten now and broad.

" No," said dad. His breath was coming short. He looked right poorly, but he insisted on taking his share. Perhaps it was pride that made him go on, all the beasts he'd dragged across the hill in his time.

They left the hind below the tall rock that was

called the Steeple where the pony-man would easily find her.

" What's up, Dad? " asked Geordie. He was worried, never having seen him anything but strong.

" It's just a wee pain," said dad, putting his hand on his chest. " Here. It's better now."

They cut straight across the hill towards the track which was the quickest way home. The wind was higher now, and the rain came flat across the moor from the East; first rain, then a few wet flakes amongst it, then heavy sleet, then snow. It was half-past three when they reached the track. Half an hour should see them back in the sheltered valley.

But dad stumbled once and went on and stumbled again. His face was grey.

Geordie could see now that there was something bad the matter with him. It wasn't just a man of fifty tired after pulling a heavy beast. He touched his arm. " Take a wee rest again, Dad," he said.

Dad shook his head, eyes fixed along the track. He looked pinched and shut off. " Down before the snow," he muttered.

" Hold my arm then, Dad," said Geordie. He was thinking hard, wondering what was the best thing to do if dad couldn't walk it. Two miles to go yet, downhill, but rough.

Dad held his arm, getting heavier; but when he did flop, it was sudden, right across the cart rut in the wet snow, and he lay still.

Geordie bent over him. " Get the pony," said dad in a wheezy whisper.

Get the pony? Half an hour down, an hour, perhaps two hours till they could fetch him; and the snow heavy and the wind. No, that was too long.

" I'll carry you, Dad," said Geordie. He dropped the rifle in its cover beside the track.

Dad said nothing. He closed his eyes, out in a faint or maybe something worse. Geordie didn't know. All he knew was that he must get him down quickly.

He got his father's slack body over his shoulders in a fireman's lift. It was hard getting up with all that weight, for dad was a heavy man, bigger than Geordie himself by a good bit. But he managed it. The walking wasn't too bad at first, not until the track became steep and he had to watch his feet in the deep ruts and on the tussocks, and that weight bearing down on him.

It's a good thing I'm strong, he thought. It's a good thing I worked with Samson these two years. But then it was bad too, him using the strength he'd built up just for to carry his dad off the hill, and dad right sick, dad going to die perhaps. It was a poor way to use the strength you were learning.

There was an ache going right through Geordie's body now, through his shoulders and his lungs and his legs. He couldn't hardly bear it. The strength was nearly out of him, but he kept on down the slope, thinking of only one thing—that he mustn't stumble. Over the last crest, rain instead of snow, the valley murky down there, smoke going flat from the chimney of their own cottage, of dad's cottage; across the flat ground half blind and wondering if he'd ever manage it. But he did manage it, and he slumped with a thud against the door.

Mum came then. Geordie gasped out to her what had happened.

"Better now," dad muttered, but he didn't look much better. "A good laddie, our Geordie."

Mum got dad by the shoulders. "The doctor told ye, Jock," she scolded, "but ye wouldna' heed him." Mum sounded right angry in her worry. It was the first Geordie had ever heard of dad and the doctor.

They got him into bed, and Geordie went the mile on his bike to call the doctor on the telephone. He was about all in by then.

The doctor came a second time next morning. He was looking at dad in the bed in the kitchen. The district nurse was in there too. Mum and Geordie waited in the Room. Geordie never liked the Room, never felt comfortable in there amongst the leathery chairs and polished lino and lace curtains. He never liked the new strange smelly dampness of it. He hated it this morning.

Doctor Murdoch came through in the end. He was a small grey man, getting old. He closed the door behind him.

" Your husband's bad, Mistress MacTaggart," he said, blunt but kind. Doctor Murdoch always told it out straight; that was the reputation he had. " Him with a weak heart. He should have listened to what I said. But it's not only his heart now. He's got pneumonia from the exposure." He stopped and looked at mum.

" Is there a chance, Doctor? " she said. Mum's face was calm and her voice was ordinary. It was only just a tiny trembling of her lip for a second that told Geordie what she was feeling.

" There's a chance," he said, looking at her again. " But small."

The nurse came through then. " He wants to see Geordie," she said to the doctor.

" Go on, Geordie," said Doctor Murdoch,

putting his hand on Geordie's shoulder and giving him a wee pat. " Just stay a minute."

Geordie went into the kitchen. He didn't like the smell in there either; some stuff they'd been rubbing into dad's chest; and there was the feeling of fever in the air.

Dad was breathing short and shallow. There was colour back in his face, but it wasn't the right kind of colour.

" Hallo, Dad," said Geordie, not liking in a way to be near his sick dad, but not showing it.

" None the worse, Geordie? " said dad, opening his eyes.

" I'm fine," Geordie said. He was stiff from top to toe as a matter of fact.

" Go away up and get the rifle."

Geordie had forgotten all about the rifle on the hill. Think of dad remembering that!

" And Geordie! "

" Yes, Dad? "

" You ken the Black Watch kilt? "

" Ay."

" You're to keep it. Maybe you'll use it one day."

" Right, Dad." He couldn't hardly speak with dad choosing that way to say he thought he was going to die. Dad had been a sergeant in the Black Watch. Sometimes he'd go to where the kilt was hanging, and take a wee look at it, getting a memory of the times he'd had in the regiment.

" Get the rifle and clean it right," said dad. He spoke sharply so it was a surprise.

Geordie took a look at dad's lined face on the pillow. He went out of the room, out of the house and straight up the hill path.

He had just reached the fork when he heard Jean calling to him. She was coming along from the garden direction, wearing her old waterproof; it was another dirty day. Geordie stopped.

" Where are you going, Geordie? " she asked when she was close. Jean looked very young in that old coat, with the rain on her face.

" Up the hill for the rifle," said Geordie.

" Can I come? "

He didn't answer; and she fell in beside him and they started climbing. They went quite a long way before she spoke.

Then she said quietly: " I heard tell the way you carried your dad off the hill. You're strong, Geordie."

Geordie's answer came into his mind and was spoken before he knew. He hadn't been angry for a long time, not since he could remember almost, but suddenly he felt bitter at her and at everything. " There's uses for elephants," he said, looking straight ahead at the wet muck on the path.

He wished he hadn't said that. He wished he hadn't said it to Jean, and her only joking last summer, and dad sick down there.

" Och, Geordie," she said, and she put out her hand and gave his a squeeze and took it away again.

It wasn't a long walk up to where the rifle lay among the heather. Geordie slung it over his shoulder and they started back again. The wind was behind them now, and it was a loose easy swing down the hill.

" He said I was to keep his Black Watch kilt," Geordie said. He couldn't hold everything bottled up inside him any more.

" He's real bad then, Geordie? "

" Ay, he's bad. The doctor says it's a small chance." The tears welled up in Geordie's eyes. " I never knew dad's heart was bad. I don't want dad's kilt. I want my dad."

She took his hand again and held it. So they went hand in hand.

" The kilt'll be a thing he's proud of," she said.

" That's right," said Geordie, not able to see straight, but getting comfort from Jean's warm wet hand.

" I'll come as far as the house," she said. They

went on together till they stood outside the grey cottage in the grey November morning.

" I hope your dad pulls through, Geordie," she said.

But Geordie shivered. He saw death in the wet brown bracken and the leaves. He felt it all round him. He felt it struggling to enter his father's house; and he knew from her troubled eyes that Jean could feel it too. They were young Highland people, quiet people who understand the quiet places.

* 4 *

GEORDIE'S fears were right, for the next day his father died, and there was a dark time for mum and Geordie in the cottage, being taciturn people and not well able to take comfort from the sharing of grief.

But dad got a great funeral. He had been a man respected in the countryside, and other men came from the town, from the big valley, from the narrow glens, rich and poor and all dressed in sober black to give him a good send-off.

The kirk was packed. There was a creaking of assent among the pews when Reverend MacNab paid tribute. "He was a good man, and his memory will be an example for us."

Then afterwards, when the simple words had been spoken and the first earth lay upon the coffin, Geordie stood for the men to grasp his hand in silence and go their way.

Sorrow and responsibility had come early for Geordie.

But he was young and there was work to do and
no time for moping even if Geordie had been a
moper which he was not. You couldn't feel sad
exactly when every step you took about the place,
and every job you did, there was dad's voice coming
up from before and telling you the right way of it.
You couldn't feel he was gone altogether.

Geordie didn't get a word of instructions until
Friday night missing one, which was dad's night
for seeing the Laird. So he spruced himself
up with a necktie and all, and went over to the
Bighoose. He went through into the kitchen where
Mistress Robertson was getting the Laird's dinner
ready. There wasn't much love lost between
Geordie and Mistress Robertson on account of a
few things which had happened in the past, but
she wasn't bad to him that night.

" I will inform the Laird," she said politely, and
cleaned her hands on her apron and went off along
the back passage.

Geordie was a bit nervous, him getting the
Laird's instructions for the first time; although
naturally he'd seen him at the time of the funeral.
He had to wait a bit till Mistress Robertson came
back.

" Come in, George."

Geordie went into the study. The Laird stood up

at the desk and came round. He was an awful
long lanky chap, just about as thin as a rake, and
untidy because of having no wife perhaps. He had
on his old kilt which was in shreds at the bottom,
and drooped down the back of his spindly legs,
and was faded to the colour of old rope. He had a
great big moustache stretching across his thin face.
You wouldn't think he was twenty-fifth in his line,
which was what dad said he was. And dad said,
he may seem comical with the droopy kilt and all
the queer notions he has, but he's no fool, Geordie,
let me tell you.

Geordie was thinking of all this when the Laird
surprised him by shaking hands and going back
and sitting down at his desk.

"Well, George," he said. "Very sad about
your father. He was a good friend." The Laird
spoke like a foreigner, but of course if it was twenty-
five generations he was maybe less of a foreigner
than Geordie was himself. Perhaps it was the
schooling he'd had away down in England.

Geordie gulped at the mention of dad. He was
at the stage when it was all right if folk didn't speak
about it.

But the Laird was going on: " I'm glad you're
here to take on from him. That is, of course, if
you want to. I hope you do."

" I don't mind," said Geordie, which is Scottish for I'd like to.

" Well, that's fine," said the Laird, and he went on to tell Geordie that he would be second to Frazer, the man who worked the other beat, and he would get a raise in wages but not much till he was older, and what birds had he seen on the hill, and when would he be through with the hinds, chopping and changing from this to that so it was hard to follow. You got out of breath listening to the Laird, and all his talk was cut off like a telegram. Birds and trees were the things he was keenest on. He spent half his days with the binoculars round his neck, carrying the patent gadget he had for stripping branches off his trees, and a small axe for thinning.

" No shooting kestrels now, George. I don't allow them to be killed. Harmless hawks, falcons to be accurate. They're beneficial as a matter of fact. I saw one up at the young spruce plantation yesterday. Talking of plantations, I can't get a word of sense out of the Forestry Commission about the new one I want to plant above Egypt's Camp. They're no damned good, those people. Costs me a fortune to plant anything; and that's what they want, isn't it? The country's going to pot, damned government, damned everything. What are your politics, George? "

Geordie jumped. He was in a daze by this time. " What's that, sir? "

" Your politics. What are you, a Communist or a Conservative, or what? "

Geordie was outraged. " A Cawmunist? " Perhaps the Laird was just joking; you couldn't tell. Dad was a Liberal. " I'm a Liberal," he said.

" Good for you, George. All sensible people are Liberals. Not enough sensible people."

The Laird stopped a minute and smiled. " Don't be alarmed, George," he said. " I always drool on. My goodness you're getting to be a big fellow. I hear you've been taking courses and everything. Well, don't overdo it."

Geordie felt himself getting red. How did the old chap know that?

" That reminds me, you'll need a tweed suit." He took a piece of paper and wrote on it for a minute. " Here, take this to Mr. McKerchar."

The note said:

" DEAR MR. McK.
    Wd. u pl. make knick. suit for Geo. MacT.
                    Yrs
                            G. F. C. P.
P.S.—Big tucks because rate of growth phenom."

Geordie couldn't hardly make head nor tail of it.

That was another one of the Laird's queernesses, writing abbreviated for efficiency and time-saving. Folk would take days to make his notes out sometimes.

" Well, George, I'm lucky to have you. You'll have to be good to be as good as your father. Come on Fridays or any time. Good night."

" Good night, sir," said Geordie and made his way to the door.

" Oh, George," said the Laird, thinking of something else to say.

" Yessir ? "

" How's Jean ? Nice girl that."

" Jean's fine," said Geordie, and went blushing along the dark passage. Maybe there was something in what dad used to say about the Laird being no fool under all his daft notions.

Well, time flew by—that long winter and a summer, and the pain of dad's dying eased even for mum, and another year till the spring came again and Geordie had his eighteenth birthday, and still he grew. The days when he was Wee Geordie seemed far away. Now he was Big Geordie, so big that people would stop in the street on the days when he was in town and would take another look

D

to see if what they saw was true. But he went on developing himself; it had become like a habit. Wanting to be big is the same as everything else; once get started wanting and you're never satisfied. And you keep on with the exercises, thinking its them that makes you grow; although perhaps God would have made you just as big a fellow if you'd never done a single one of those contortions.

This was a Saturday afternoon, a day quite like that Saturday four years ago when Geordie had his first letter with the course from Henry Samson. When he got back for dinner, mum said, " There's a letter for you, Geordie."

He took a look at the postmark. " Wadsworth," it was. Geordie left the letter till after dinner. He wasn't one of those people who tear them open on first receipt. He liked to let them simmer, and then he would read them in good time when he was comfortable.

So afterwards he took the letter outside, sat down on the bench in the sunlight, and opened it up to see what Henry Samson had to say.

" DEAR GEORDIE,

I am in receipt of yours of 30th ult. and send thanks for £1 in payment of dues for my Master's Course. Your success with the Beginner's

Course and the Advanced Course has been splendid.

The highest praise I can say is that you are a credit to Henry Samson.

You will observe that the Master's Course is more flexible than the first two. It is designed in accordance with my guiding rule: First Achieve Balanced Development; then Specialize. Don't put the cart before the horse in other words. Well, now you are ready for specializing, Geordie. I have studied the measurements you sent (very spectacular improvement!) and it seems to me that your height and great shoulder and bicep development fits you to be a Shot-Putter. Did you ever try that Line? The paths of training lead but to the object, so why not make your object Shot-Putting?

Yours truly

HENRY SAMSON

P.S.—You could toss the Caber for variety."

That was another lovely letter from Mr. Samson. These four years he'd treated Geordie like a favourite pupil, always writing promptly, and sending a fine new picture of himself every Christmas.

Geordie had never thought very much about putting the shot. He'd often tossed boulders, of course. That was part of his general training. But he'd never done it special; he'd never done it scientific, you might say. Now he began to think it over, and the more he thought about the idea the better he liked it. Yes, shot-putting was a fine specialisation. It might easily turn out to be his object in the Master's Course.

He felt warm and lazy there in the sun with the week's work ended and the chaffinch pouring out his voice from up the holly tree; but Geordie never allowed himself any softness, so he got up and went to look for a round stone to use as a shot.

He found a good round one and balanced it up and down in his right hand and putted it away in a practice. It didn't go very comfortably. Geordie drew a line across the grass with the heel of his boot and practised with that as a starting place. He got better after a few shots. " Practice makes perfect," he muttered to himself, and kept on at it. That was another one of Mr. Samson's watchwords.

" Hallo, Geordie," said a familiar high-pitched voice.

Geordie turned round. It was Reverend MacNab, the minister, sitting on his bike on the road with the toes of his boots touching the ground. He had on his black suit and his black hat and the usual cheery grin on his red face.

" Hallo, Minister," said Geordie, a bit sheepish at being caught playing with stones and him grown up.

Mr. MacNab got off his bike and came over. He was quite a pal of Geordie's in a way, not that you could be real pally with a chap who had to swear off sin. But certainly the holiness didn't hang heavy on the minister. He could have a hearty laugh for all his arsey-tarsey collar.

He let his bike fall, put the hat over one of the handlebars, and stood with his hands in his trouser pockets. His face was all sweaty and polished from riding uphill.

" So you've got on to putting the weight, Geordie," he said. " I'll watch you."

Geordie cursed inside. He didn't want to go making an exhibition of himself at something he hadn't learned the way of. But he marked the starting line again which was getting smudged, and took a few more puts.

" Here, Geordie," said the minister. " Hold it like this, close into your shoulder, wrist straight, so it goes with the force of your body."

Geordie did what he said, but not very willingly. What would a minister know about shot-putting, and him just a wee bit of a chap beside Geordie? But it did seem to go better with the stone held close.

" Hold it in your fingers," said MacNab; and that didn't do any harm either.

" Too low, Geordie. Throw higher. You know I believe you'd make a shot-putter if you learned how to do it."

" That's what I'm going to do," said Geordie. He dropped the stone with a thud on the grass. He was a bit fed-up.

" I'll have a competition with you," said MacNab. He took off his jacket and waistcoat. He had on a pair of bright blue braces which didn't seem right somehow. The minister was a whole head below Geordie, not more than five foot eight perhaps, but broad; you could see he had strong wee arms on him when he rolled up his sleeves.

" You go first, Geordie," he said.

Geordie did a good one, the best yet. They marked the spot with a stick.

Then it was Reverend MacNab's turn. He nestled the big stone in his shoulder, and swung his left leg back and forward getting balance. Then he launched himself at the line and the whole of his body spun in a half turn and the stone flew up and away and over and down a good six foot beyond Geordie's.

That was one of the biggest surprises of Geordie's life.

The minister had been smiling all the time before, but now he bubbled over with delight. He laughed with a high cackle, hee hee hee, till even the chaffinch stopped singing; and he bent over in his mirth and gasped for breath. He was just about busting he was so pleased with himself.

And Geordie began to laugh too. He couldn't help it, with the wee fella' giving him such a beating.

He forgot to speak polite. " I didna' ken . . ." he began. " Where did ye . . .? "

" I used to do it at the Varsity in Glasgow," said Mr. MacNab. He was still chuckling. " Forty foot was my best. I'm too short to be really good at it; for the top class, I mean."

He put on his waistcoat and jacket again; and he was quite serious for once. " You know, Geordie," he said, " if you had speed you might be a great shot-putter. Now I'll tell you what you ought to do for practice." And he explained to Geordie about speed across the circle and strength and co-ordination.

" You couldn't give me a lesson whiles, could you, Mr. MacNab? " asked Geordie.

The minister's face lit up again. " I'd like fine to do that, Geordie. I'm often past here on my bike in the evenings. I'll just stop by and see if you're about the place."

" Well, thanks," said Geordie, still a bit stupefied how a wee chap, not so young either, and a minister to make it worse, could skin the hide off him in putting a stone. It was good nobody had been watching. If Jean had seen what happened, would she have had a laugh!

" I've a sixteen-pound shot at the Manse. You can have that, Geordie."

" Och, thanks," said Geordie again.

" Cheerio, Geordie. I'll have to get away after my flock now."

" Cheeri-ta-ta, Mr. MacNab."

He could hear the minister giggling away to himself for quite a distance along the road.

And that was how Geordie got started on the shot-putting.

* 5 *

REVEREND MACNAB sat comfortably on a rock. He had his black minister's hat tilted over his eyes on account of the evening sun; underneath the hat his face was pink and cheery just like usual. Bess the Labrador, she was lying beside him, old Bess now with a grey muzzle. She was a sober dog, and so much respected that she could have a wee bit hunt after a rabbit whenever she took the fancy, and Geordie wouldn't stop her like he would the others.

But Bess wasn't thinking of rabbits. She had her head down on her paws, and she and Mr. MacNab were watching Geordie intently while he practised shot-putting in the old stone quarry. Summer had come round again, and Mr. MacNab cast his mind back with satisfaction to the day a year ago when he had first given Geordie a few tips. He remembered his muckle lumbering then, the great strength wasted in clumsy effort; and he compared that with what he saw this evening: with the speed and the control and the economy of power. Mr. MacNab liked to make simple analogies from the Book. One jumped into his mind now. Last year Geordie had been a clumsy Goliath, but to-day he was a giant David, light of foot for all his size, limber as David with his sling.

" Not bad, Geordie," he said, concealing his pleasure; for understatement is next to Godliness in those parts.

Geordie flicked the shot from one hand to the other, waiting for the Reverend to tell him what to do next. He had taken off his shirt for freedom, and he stood with his heavy boots planted wide, muscles rippling. He looked the simple and kindly giant that he was.

The minister stood up. " I'll put the peg at forty-six feet," he said. They measured out the distance and put in the peg.

" Now try one full strength, Geordie—weight forward. Try to get that spin from your hips a little faster yet."

Geordie stood in the circle with the curved board in front of him. He cradled the shot in his fingers, nestled it close into the hollow of his neck, swung and balanced, bent and straightened, bent again and held his breath and unleashed himself in a ferocious glide across the circle.

He knew it was to be a good one before the shot left his fingers. It thudded down beyond the peg.

Mr. MacNab burst out laughing. "That's the best yet, Geordie," he said. "No more to-night." Bess wagged her tail.

Geordie pulled his shirt on again. He was pleased with that last one.

"Saturday first's the Drumfechan Games," said the minister casually.

"Is that so?" said Geordie, doing up the buttons. He'd never bothered much with watching the games.

"If you did another one like that you'd win the shot-putting easy."

"Och," said Geordie. Practising was one thing, learning to do it good so you felt you were well-developed. But doing it in a competition, that was another. What was the use of a competition anyway? "I'm no keen on competeetions."

"There's no harm in them, Geordie." The minister looked hopefully at him. "I'd like fine to see you beat some of those big police fellas."

"Would it sairve a purpose?"

The minister sighed and got to his feet. He dearly wanted to see Geordie perform in the Games, but he knew his man too well to press the idea.

"I must get away home," he said. "Just you

think it over about the Games, Geordie. It would be good practice and you might get some tips. Good night to you." He turned and went down the path.

"Cheeribye, Mr. MacNab," said Geordie. He had a few snares to look at on his way home, so he set off across the steep grass fields which lay along the side of the valley. It was a hot evening for July, still and oppressive, and the clouds were gathering in the south-west, creeping up indigo-black towards the sun. He heard a partridge call twice below him—chettiriya, chettiriya. The noise rang crisply and sweetly through the stillness. It was a lovely sound on an evening when thunder was in the air. Then the clouds climbed over the sun, and the blackness of them faded into brown, and a tickle of wind puffed from the east.

"We'll get a storm," Geordie said aloud, but he did not listen for the mutter of thunder and he did not watch the dark sky; he was thinking of something altogether different, something bright and delightful, more important than shot-putting, more important even than work. He was thinking of Jean, wondering if he would be lucky to-night and see her on his way home.

He only got one rabbit. They were always dour in thundery weather. Geordie took the wire off the swollen head, rounded the noose again and set it over the run. Then he slit one of the back legs, crossed the other through it and went on with the rabbit dangling from his hand.

Most evenings Jean would be out with the Scottie at this time, giving her stubby black dog a walk. Geordie had no use for pet dogs that didn't work, not much more use than for cats which were the worst hunters of all; but Jean's wee Sandy was a part of Jean, so Geordie didn't grudge him a hunt as long as he stuck to rabbits.

He was in the woods again when he heard the terrier yap. Bess stood still a moment and listened to the hoarse barking. " Come away, Bess," said Geordie, quickening his pace.

They came on Jean round a corner. She put her fingers to her mouth and gave a piercing whistle. It was always a surprise to Geordie to hear a man's whistle come from a lassie's lips, and her so slim and dark and bonny, and it was him taught her to do it long ago. He didn't speak till he was close. Bess came along sedate and respectable to heel.

" Hallo, Jean," said Geordie.

She gave a start and turned round. Then she blushed. It was just a soft quick tide of colour which came and went, but it pleased Geordie. It gave him a great feeling to think she'd blush for him. She was frowning, though.

" Sandy's away again," said Jean. She whistled a second time. The yapping sounded once more. Then there was silence. It had been quiet outside on the fields, but here among the trees you could feel it all round you. You could feel there was just the trees and the silence and you and Jean and nothing else in the world.

" The wee devil's hunting," Geordie said severely, watching her. Sometimes if he got a word in first, it would stop Jean from sharpening her wits on him. She did that an awful lot nowadays. But he failed this time.

" What d'ye think he's doing, you . . . you great muckle Man Mountain? " She eyed him sharply, hotly almost, and looked away again among the trees.

Sandy came back then, scrambling over the fallen trunks and through the bracken. He was a square wee dog, about as broad as he was long. He looked pleased with himself and said howd'youdo to Geordie and to Bess and the rabbit in Geordie's hand. Then he lay down with his tongue hanging out, panting.

Geordie looked at Jean. He could never take his eyes off her when they were together; he could never have the picture of her oval face clear enough in his mind; it was a new miracle each time he saw her.

" What were you doin', Geordie? " Perhaps she said it for something to say; perhaps she was a little shy of him too.

" I was practising wi' the minister."

" Was he pleased at you? " The glint always came into Jean's eye when Geordie spoke of his exercises or his shot-putting.

" Ay, he was pleased."

" That's a rare waste of time, hurling a cannon-ball. What use is it? " She looked up at him with her grey eyes under the dark lashes, half mocking.

" The minister wants me for to enter in the Drumfechan Games."

" And will you? "

" I don't think it. I've no mind for compe-teetions."

" Why not? Competitions is more sense than jest throwing by yourself."

Geordie suppressed a sigh. Whatever he did seemed to be wrong to Jean. " I don't fancy the idea. What for would I throw against other chaps? "

" What for did you learn it then? "

Geordie thought a bit. " I learnt it for the sake of learning, as part of the programme like."

" But do ye not want to do it better'n the other men? " For some reason Jean seemed to be keen on the idea of the games.

Geordie made a pattern on the path with his foot. " I'd like fine to do it well," he said. " I'm no caring how other folk does it."

She turned to face him. Jean was a good-sized lassie, but she was small and mysterious beside him. The soft curves of her body were something he thought of, but humbly.

" Go on, Geordie," she said. " You do it."

He shook his head. " I'm no keen."

Just then the thunder rumbled. It rumbled far away, but it came into the wood too, so that it was in there with him and Jean. The green of the moss was dark now on the ground, and Jean's face was shadowy.

" Please, Geordie! " She came a little closer to him. " Just for me, Geordie."

How could he refuse? He never did understand the way Jean thought, but he loved her and he had no heart to say no.

" Will you be there, Jean? "

She smiled then. It was the soft smile he remembered from the time dad died. It was the smile she had given him a few times since.

" I'll be there, Geordie."

The thunder was closer now, and lightning flickered its dead light among the trees. The first heavy drops of rain were pattering on the leaves high above them.

" We'll need to hurry," said Jean, but she still stood close to him. They were caught in the magic and the burden of the storm.

That was how it was when the bright flash came and the moment's silence and the great cannons of the sky. That was what gave Geordie the courage he had never found with her before.

He put his spare hand round Jean's waist and bent and kissed her on the lips. It was a clumsy kiss, awkward as the first kisses of a boy and a girl are sure to be; but it sent a flood of delight through him.

He could feel Jean shiver in his arms. She clung softly to him for a moment while the rain fell coldly on their hair. " My wee Geordie," she murmured, and laughed so close to him it was like himself laughing. " Do ye need to hold the rabbit too? "

He laughed and let it drop and put both his arms round her and they were together and he knew everything that had happened and would happen.

E

She broke from him without another word, and ran off along the murky path, dark hair flying, the small black dog scurrying at her heels. Then they were out of sight.

Geordie walked quickly, but he was soaked through by the time he had given old Bess a rub and put her in her kennel; he paid no heed to the rain or the lightning, for his mind was a riot. Geordie was bemused; that was the truth of it.

" Away and get changed, Geordie," said mum. " And don't bring those wet feet into my kitchen." She treated him like he was still a wee boy.

Geordie took his boots off and went upstairs to the room where he had always slept. He got into dry things and came down again and sat beside the fire. It was quite chilly now that the storm had come. It was still raining outside, but the thunder had moved down the valley.

He read the paper for a bit. Mum was doing some ironing.

" I saw the minister come by," she said. " How did ye get on the night? "

" It was my best yet," said Geordie. " Reverend MacNab was pleased."

" Well, that's fine."

" They've got me persuaded to enter the Games on Saturday first."

" Who's they? " said mum, turning to look at him, smiling for some reason. Mum's hair was grey now; she was a comfortable looking body, aye laughing at something.

" Just the minister," said Geordie from behind his paper; and there was silence again.

" What'll you wear, Geordie? " She had stopped ironing and was watching him.

" For the Games, Mum? "

She nodded.

" I dinna ken. Just the best plus fours. What else would I wear? "

" You could wear dad's kilt. The kilt's right for shot-putting." Mum's face was serious.

" Whit way would I wear the kilt, Mum? I never did afore, 'n it's a sodjers kilt."

" It's your dad's Black Watch kilt that he left you special."

" Och, Mum! It be ower small."

" I'll get it the now," said mum firmly, and she went out of the kitchen. She came back in a minute with the dark kilt.

" There's three inches I could let down," she said. " Take your breeks off now, laddie."

Geordie took his breeks off and stood in his shirt. He grumbled away to himself, but it wasn't any good arguing the toss with mum once she had her mind made up. She fitted the kilt round his waist and did up the straps. They went in at the last hole. The kilt came high above his knees.

"That'll be fine," said mum, going all the way round him, pulling and prodding at him like he was a big sack.

"What'll the Black Watch say? They'll no allow it."

"I'll take the green flashes off," said mum. "Then they'll not mind. Onyway, they'd like fine to see a braw laddie in his dad's kilt."

Geordie made a last protest. "But I dinna' want to wear the kilt, Mum."

"It's what your dad would have liked. Take it off now, Geordie and I'll get it let out."

So that was that. Geordie loosed the kilt and put his breeks back on again. He was an awful simple lump of clay in a woman's hands, was Geordie.

⋆ 6 ⋆

MUM took a last look at Geordie and gave his kilt some tugs to get it hanging even all the way round.

"That's fine, Geordie," she said. "Do yer best now, and mind what I said about being careful how you sit."

"Och, Mum!"

He set off along the road towards Drumfechan. It was only three miles away. On an ordinary day he would have taken his bike, but there were several reasons why the kilt and the bike didn't go together, anyway not for an inexperienced man.

It still felt a bit strange on him, tight round his stomach and flapping round his knees, but he practised the swing of it, giving a wee jerk to his bottom each time he took a step. After a mile the knack began to come to him, and the pleats swung rhythmically across the back of his knees.

Geordie was wearing his best tweed jacket, a

shirt and a tie, stockings and boots, so what with that and the kilt he made a fine figure.

Two charabancs passed him. Then he heard a third one coming; but it slowed up.

It was a big red bus. The driver leaned over to the window nearest Geordie.

" Am I right for Drumfeckan? " he asked.

" Straight ahead," said Geordie. " Turn left before the loch."

" Want a lift? "

Geordie hesitated, sensing the rows of feminine eyes at the windows. Well, it would save time. He climbed into the bus and sat beside the driver. It was a busload of lassies, and they were chattering away like lassies do. But they were suddenly silent except for stifled giggles and whispers.

Geordie was shy in there with all those females. Not that he could see them behind him, but he felt them all right, and he knew they were watching him. Also he heard what one whispered to another. " D'y'ever see such a lovely boy, Kate? "

Geordie felt himself going red all over. The redness tingled on the back of his neck, so he had to say something to hide his confusion.

" Did you come far? "

" From Newcastle," said the driver, raising his

voice above the engine. " We're on a week-end tour."

Newcastle was down in England somewhere. " That's a long step," said Geordie.

The driver leaned over and spoke more quietly. " Thirty-two o' them, and just me. Can you beat it ? "

The lassies had begun to chatter again behind Geordie and he was able to relax. Soon the bus was running down into the village.

The driver raised his voice to a commanding bellow. " Attention, please, ladies! " The ladies were silent. " We are now approachin' Drumfeckan. We shall stop one hour at the Highland Games. Then all aboard for Strathpeffer. Don't be late please, ladies! "

Even if the chap was only an Englishman, Geordie couldn't help admiring him. He handled his ladies with the greatest self-assurance.

The bus stopped beside the field. " Thanks," said Geordie, and he jumped out quickly, hoping that no one would see him leaving a bus with thirty-two girls in it.

But no one seemed to notice, and he got in free at the gate because he was a competitor.

The Drumfechan Games were held in a field beside the loch. They weren't grand Highland

Games like you'd find at Braemar or the like; but
local. There were bicycle races and highland
dancing and running and jumping, flowers and veg.
in a big marquee, everybody dressed up in his best
clothes and sweaty on account of the hot sun and
the loch as calm as a millpond, and an Eyetalian
chap selling ices; N. Valente his name was. He
looked a right Eyetie, but he had a broad Scotch
voice on account of him being the second generation.

Away over in the far corner under the big Scots
pine the piping was going on. It was the pibroch,
three judges sitting at a table, and a lonely piper
playing his lament and moving slow before them.
It was a dirgey sound, not great music to a stranger's
ears, but sad and beautiful to the Highland people.
That was the music which lay in below their minds.
It went with them to the high glens, or down from
the hill when they drove the black-faced sheep to
market.

Everybody was having a fine time, although you
wouldn't know it from the serious faces. Almost
everybody; Geordie himself was not very happy.
He was grumbling away inside because mum had
made him wear dad's kilt, and him wondering if it
sat right about him, and knowing his knees were
too white for a real kilt-wearing man, and some of
the boys pulling his leg on account of them remem-

bering him as Wee Geordie in the school and seeing
what a great lump of a Jock he was now, and
seeing too that the kilt was foreign to him.

And where was Jean? Geordie kept looking
round to see if he could find her, but she was
nowhere about. He hadn't seen her since Monday
when the storm was, and he had kissed her. He
felt a tingle all over at the memory of that. Perhaps
Jean wouldn't come; perhaps she never wanted to
see him after that kiss.

The shot-putting wasn't due for half an hour yet.
Geordie walked past the wooden platform where
the wee lassies were dancing the sword dance. He
watched one of them for a minute, dressed up in her
kilt and diced hose and bonnet and all, light as a
fairy on her feet, pattering like magic over the
crossed swords and never a touch, hands looped
gracefully, finishing in a flurry of the quick reel-
time, and standing back, and marching like a small
soldier off the boards, and the next one taking her
place.

That brought him to the big marquee. He went
inside. All the noises were muted in there, and the
people went slowly along one side where the flowers
were banked, and back the other past the vegetables,
and tickets beside the exhibits—First, Second,
Third, Highly Commended, Special Award.

" Fine day for it, Geordie," said somebody just inside the tent.

" Ay," said Geordie. " Fine day for it."

He went on past the flowers. It was very hot in there, stuffy too, and the smell was a mixture of sweet peas and onions and Sunday clothes and soap and sweat, a special mixed-up smell you got on the one day in the year.

Mr. Donaldson, Jean's dad, was standing at the far end. He was wearing a blue suit. He looked very respectable with his bowler hat and his red face and his committee badge. He was chief judge of vegetables.

" It's a fine show, Mr. Donaldson," said Geordie, not knowing if it was fine or not; but it looked good to him and anyway Mr. Donaldson was Jean's dad and Geordie wished to be agreeable.

" Not bad, Geordie," said Mr. Donaldson judiciously, casting his eye up and down the vegetables —the fine clusters of onions, and the cauliflowers like white pincushions, the green peas in flat bowls, and the strawberries so big and red they made your mouth water. " I obsairve a slight improvement over last year."

" How's things in the garden, Mr. Donaldson? " asked Geordie, just for something to say.

He wondered if Jean could have come with her dad, but he didn't dare to ask.

" No bad . . . no bad . . ." said Mr. Donaldson. He generally said things twice over. " The Cushies is botherin' me again. I'd be obliged if you'd shoot a few." He looked sternly at Geordie for a moment, saying but not saying that a young keeper couldn't hardly be expected to do his job properly.

The Cushies, the wood pigeons, were an old trouble between the gardener and the gamekeeper, them and the rabbits and the pheasants; and the Donaldsons' cat hunting about the place. There were grouses and grumbles both ways, but Geordie was too young to give Mr. Donaldson any lip, even though if he hadn't been Jean's dad, Geordie would have liked to express his thoughts. What harm would a few Cushies do?

" I'll attend to it, Mr. Donaldson," he said respectfully, and went back past the vegetables, wondering how Jean ever got such a stuck-up old chap for a dad. He was a good gardener, though, or so folk said.

Outside it was cool after the tent. Geordie cast his eyes about again for Jean, but he couldn't see her anywhere. Come to think of it, he wasn't so sure he did want to see her, him feeling awkward and wishing he'd never agreed to enter in the Shot-

Putting against all the Pros from Dundee and Aberdeen and other big places.

He thought maybe he'd go down to hear the piping; so he skirted the field. A bicycle race was taking place at the moment. They bumped past him on the grass. They were tough boys, those, bent earnestly over the handlebars, jostling one another and cursing fit to beat the band.

The Pibroch was still going on. Geordie stopped a short distance from the piper, who was nothing special as a performer. The Laird was head judge. He looked restless ʼin behind the table, darting glances here and there. When he spotted Geordie he got up from his chair and came right over. The two other judges looked anxiously at him and at one another. Then one of them went and stopped the piper. The sound of the pibroch died and the air moaned out of the bag and the piper didn't look well pleased at being interrupted. But nobody else seemed to mind. When the Laird judged anything it was sure to be a pantomime. He'd do whatever came into his mind, and bye and bye somebody might get him back to doing what he shouldn't have stopped doing.

" Hallo, George," he said. The Laird had his usual droopy kilt festooned about him and the bonnet perched on top of his wispy hair and the long shepherd's crook in his hand. He was Chieftain of the Games this year, so he wore a badge with that printed as large as life on it.

" Hallo, sir," said Geordie, a bit uncomfortable that it should have been him who attracted the Laird's attention and stopped the piping.

" Damned bad piper, that fellow. I say, George, you look well in the kilt. Wish I had a backside like yours to make mine swing."

Geordie blushed to the roots of his hair. The Laird was speaking loudly, and Geordie was sure everyone at the Games could hear his remarks.

" Here, let's have a look at you." He prowled all round Geordie like a friendly collie-dog. " Your father's kilt, I suppose. You're a credit to him. Damned hot day, isn't it? You look like Bonnie Prince Charlie or young Lochinvar or gay Lothario, or Doctor Johnson in the Hebrides, no no, hardly like him."

Geordie shifted from foot to foot, wishing the Laird would go back to his judging and leave him be. But it was good of him to come up specially; and anyway Geordie was fond of the old chap even if he couldn't make head nor tail of half what he said.

" I hear you're Putting the Shot. Hope you put a pretty one. Well, I suppose I'd better get back to my judging. Is Jean here to watch you, George?"

"She was to come, sir," said Geordie. "But I haven't seen her." He was surprised at himself, taking the Laird into his confidence like; but he needed somebody to be an ally, with the hollow feeling in his stomach and perhaps Jean not coming. There wasn't much the Laird didn't understand in his own daft way.

"Don't you worry, George. Jean wouldn't miss seeing you. Take my word for it."

Just then the man with the megaphone shouted; "All competitors for Putting the Shot." So the Laird went back to the long-suffering pipers and judges, and Geordie hurried over to the shot-putting.

They were a big-looking lot of chaps clustered beside the white-painted board and circle, and solemn men most of them, being policemen. They looked veterans every one, and they eyed Geordie like he had some nerve daring to compete against them, and him just a clumsy laddie from away up a glen. There were eight altogether—four in the kilt and three in wee white pants, and Geordie in dad's kilt. That made eight. They had those light spiky shoes on, not like the tackety boots Geordie was wearing. The champion was Sergeant Hunter of the Dundee Police and he was a giant of a man, so big Geordie felt he'd go twice into him, although of course that wasn't the case; for in truth Geordie was nearly as big as Sergeant Hunter, only he felt smaller.

"Good luck, Geordie!" called Reverend MacNab from among the spectators. His face was shining with excitement, and with pleasure at the mistaken idea that it was him who'd persuaded Geordie to enter.

Geordie looked despairingly along the line of faces, but he couldn't see Jean. There wasn't a sign of her anywhere, and his heart sank and he wished he'd never been daft enough to come here and make a fool of himself.

Serjeant Hunter was first man to go. He picked the ball up in his fingers as if it was light as a turnip. As he crouched he looked more like a big sturdy bull than anything else, and he putted it away light and easy. "Forty-four foot six," said the judge and there was a ripple of clapping.

So it went on down through the eight of them, and none of the others as good as Sergeant Hunter. Geordie slipped on the grass and did thirty-nine foot, which was terrible for him.

He thought of all the minister had taught him, and he thought of Henry Samson who'd want to hear how he got on his first time out, and he re-

membered the Success Poem, and he thought of
Jean who'd promised to come and then never came,
and he felt a slow resentment at her.

The second round was worse as far as Geordie
was concerned. He tried too hard this time and
caught his foot against the board and fell forwards.
" No put," called the judge coldly. Sergeant Hunter
had raised his to forty-five, and there were two
others nearly forty-four.

Geordie caught the minister's eye. He looked
very dejected now, not exactly pale because it wasn't
in him to have a pallid face, but he was less ruddy
than usual. However, he gave Geordie a strained
smile for encouragement.

" Last round! " said the judge, and all the big
men flexed their muscles and danced a wee caper
to limber up their legs; all except Geordie who was
still trying to find Jean among the crowd.

It was just then that he saw her red tammie
bobbing down the slope. She came running, hair
flying, light of foot, pushing her way through to
the very front of the crowd.

An expectant hush had fallen over the field.
There must have been six or seven hundred there,
and they were all keen to see Sergeant Hunter
break his own record; and perhaps they were
thinking, what's oor Geordie think he's doin',

entering in a competeetion with Scotland's best?

Perhaps they mostly thought that; but Jean couldn't have, for she called across to him. It sounded as clear as a bell, did her soft Highland voice.

" Come away now, Geordie! "

His worries, his shyness, the clumsiness he was feeling—all that fell from Geordie like magic. Now that Jean was there he could hardly wait his turn. He flexed his muscles and did his own wee caper, copying the others, although truth to tell it was an ungainly caper in those heavy boots.

Sergeant raised his to forty-six foot and a half-inch, and nobody else as good as that, and Geordie's turn at last.

He picked up the shot and took position in the circle. He wasn't in a hurry. He swayed there, waiting for the right moment to come, waiting for the moment when all his body would be in balance, and him ready to bust himself for Jean who had arrived in time.

The moment came and he made the dive and the glide and the turn, and the shot left him; effortless it felt, but the whole of his great strength was piled into the tips of the fingers of his right hand. He landed well back in the circle. The shot went slowly up, spinning against the dark foliage of the

F

Scots pine, and over and down, down, down, a
clear foot beyond the blue card which marked the
Sergeant's peg.

There was a second's hush, and then great shouts;
" Guid laddie, Geordie!   Ye're braw, Geordie!
Wha' a buty! " and so on, and a thunder of clapping,
and nobody could easily believe that he had seen
Geordie MacTaggart beat Sergeant Hunter.

Even the sergeant came over and shook his hand.
He didn't look best pleased, but he wasn't a bad
sport for all the dismay in his countenance.

" Well done, young fella'," he said.   " You've
a future in shot-putting."

That pleased Geordie.   Then the minister
thumped him on the back and Jean came near with
her eyes shining.

The minister and Jean waited till the excitement
had died down.

" Geordie! " said Reverend MacNab confiden-
tially.

" Yes, Mr. MacNab? "

" Don't accept the prize money."

" Whit way, Reverend? "

" Because you'd lose your amateur status."

Geordie didn't know what difference that would
make.   However he was in no mood to question
the minister.

He and Jean wandered over together to N. Valente
to buy an ice.

" Wha'll ye hae? " said that dark Scotsman, N.
Valente.

" Twa big sliders," said Geordie. They got rare
dollops of ice cream between the wafers, like a
sandwich.

They found a place away from the crowd because
Geordie was embarrassed at all the folk coming up
to congratulate him. He and Jean sat side by side
under the pine tree, not saying a word, but eating
their ices and very happy together, each knowing
now that the other felt the same, and not wanting
anyone in the world except Geordie and Jean. It
was love, bright as a diamond, warm as the evening
sun, soft as a fluff of dandelion floating in the air,
sweet as the heather honey.

They forgot all about the time. It wasn't till
the man with the megaphone called " Geordie
MacTaggart! " in a loud voice that Geordie leapt
to his feet and hurried off to the prize giving.

He arrived panting. The other folk made a
lane for him and he went up sheepish to the table
where the Laird was giving out the prizes.

"Hallo, George," said the Laird heartily. "Where
the devil have you been? "

" I lost track o' the time," Geordie mumbled.

" Ah-hah," said the Laird, who had seen Jean arrive. " 'Twas lost with Amaryllis in the shade. That's how you lost the track of time."

Geordie wished he'd hurry up.

" First Prize Open Shot-Putting—Geordie Mac-Taggart," said the announcer.

Someone gave the Laird an envelope which he extended to Geordie.

" Is it money, sirr? "

" Is it money? Dunno. Yes, I suppose it is."

" I canna' take it, sir," said Geordie. " On account of my ammacher status."

This was a problem for the committee. No one had ever refused a money prize before. They put their heads together and held hasty consultation, the Laird making helpful suggestions and trying everyone's patience. Geordie felt awkward standing there. Perhaps he ought to get away back into the crowd.

Eventually a small silver cup was produced. It was no bigger than an egg cup.

" Here you are, George," said the Laird. " It's a small trophy for the lusty champion of Drum-fechan." He gave Geordie a very kindly smile, not daft at all.

They shook hands and Geordie retired amid cheers. Sergeant Hunter was as pleased as punch because he got the prize money Geordie wasn't able to accept. So everybody was happy, and Geordie was happiest of all.

Jean was waiting at the edge of the crowd. They walked home together, going by the old path along the hillside. What with this and that and the next thing, it was gloaming by the time they parted.

* 7 *

AS far as the games were concerned that was
Geordie's one and only appearance. The
grouse season was on, and most Saturdays the Laird
would have a shoot, so there wasn't time for much
else. Besides, as we have noticed before, Geordie
was not deeply imbued with the competitive spirit.
" Art for art's sake " would have been his motto
if he had ever heard of the expression; and even
if Jean liked the idea of him being a champion, she
didn't want her big Geordie to be going away off
to some of them fancy places where other lassies
might get their hooks into him.

Their courtship was no gallop. It was a slow
and steady wooing, you might say—holding hands
and perhaps a kiss to close the session; and the
same next time with a little progress. But everyone knew now that Geordie and Jean were going
steady.

Another winter went by, not cold as cold winters
go, but dragging on and on until at last the sun was

warm again and wild primroses flowered along the banks and the blackbird sang his song of happiness.

Then you forgot the bleakness of the winter; you forgot the wind that bit into your cheeks, the frost that bound the loch, the deadness of it all. When you were young like Geordie you forgot that easily.

For young people the year grows even as it dies; but for the old there is a sadness at each new season.

One of Geordie's many jobs was looking after the Laird's hens. Every spring some of them would go broody and sit clock-clock-clocking the whole day through in the laying boxes in the henhouse. They would brood upon a china egg for want of something better, and their eyes would be glazed with the sweet expectancy of motherhood, and the whole thing a snare and a delusion.

Well, Geordie would select the best mothers and coop them up with a setting of real eggs, and in the fullness of time the faithful clockers would have their reward.

The chickens were well ahead this year; by the middle of May they were running strongly so that

the whole of that corner of the field was a hurry
and a scurry and a cheeping of Rhode Island Reds,
which were the kind Geordie reared mostly.

He came down this evening with the mash in
one bucket and water in the other. He hadn't
quite reached the field when he saw a hawk swing
round the corner of the wood and stoop and fly off
heavily with a chicken in its talons. That was the
cunning devil Geordie had been trying to get for
two weeks. It was one of the Laird's beloved
kestrels which he always said were harmless. So
they generally were, but sometimes, if hunting was
difficult they would start the chicken habit and find
that easy; then there was nothing to do but shoot
the bird and not let on to the Laird.

The chickens were ranging wide. When they saw
Geordie they made a piping chorus, high as high,
and dropped their heads and came towards him in
a rush from every direction. They knew the hand
that bore the mash.

He went from coop to coop, putting down the
food and water. Four of the five mothers gave a
friendly clock in greeting, but the fifth was a
hellion who squawked whenever she saw him and
pecked hard if she got the chance. She was a good
mother, though; just fierce as females sometimes
are.

After Geordie had finished with the broody hens and the chickens, he went over to feed the layers. He had that done too when he heard the Laird's familiar hail. " Yoo-hoo George," it sounded across the spring evening.

Geordie turned round. The Laird was coming down the track. Reverend MacNab was with him and a couple of strangers.

He walked over to meet them. He was still annoyed about that chicken which the hawk had taken, and he debated in his mind whether to tell about it. Better not, if the Laird didn't raise the subject.

" Hallo, George," said the Laird.

" Hallo, sir," said Geordie, touching his cap with politeness. The minister and the two strangers stood in the background. They didn't look the kind of gentry you found in those parts, more slicked up like; but they were a sturdy pair of men. They were eyeing Geordie, and talking to the minister and looking back at Geordie again. For some reason the minister was excited. He had a trick of bobbing up and down on his toes when he was steamed up about anything; and he was doing that now, up and down like a jack-in-the-box, and him in his arsey-tarsey collar just as usual.

" The chickens look well, George."

" Ay, they're healthy enough, the ones I have left."   The remark slipped out.

" Did some die on you? "

" They was killed on me," said Geordie.

The Laird and Geordie were about a match in height; their shapes were totally different, of course.

" Ah ha!   Sparrow hawks or foxes? "

" Neether," said Geordie shortly.   He could still see that sickle-winged devil swooping for the chickens.

" What then, George? "

" A kestrel."

The Laird's face, which was always ruddy because of the open air life he led and the wee drams he had at night time, took on a deeper hue, purplish. That was a sign he was vexed.

" Prejudice," he muttered.   " Stuff and nonsense!   Same old story.   Couldn't be a kestrel."

" A kestrel was what it was.   I seen it take one half an hour syne."

" Bah! " said the Laird, puffing out his thin cheeks and looking as if he would explode any minute.   He glared at Geordie and Geordie glared at him.

Geordie lapsed into the third person.   " Does the Laird no believe me? "

" Don't be a fool, George! " said the Laird.

" Would the Laird take time to watch for hisself? "

The Laird said nothing.

" I'll need to shoot it then," Geordie went on remorselessly. He was more than a little annoyed with his employer, as indeed he well might be, for the Laird was a very unreasonable fellow once he mounted a hobby horse.

They were both such obstinate characters that this might have gone on much longer if Reverend MacNab had not seen fit to intervene. He cleared his throat suggestively.

Geordie and the Laird both swung on him, ready to pulverise anyone who interfered in an argument which had become almost traditional, and in a way was dear to them both. But the minister was not interfering; he was changing the subject.

" Do you have the weight down at the house, Geordie? "

" The weight? Ay, it's there." At that moment the weight was of no importance at all to him.

" I'd be much obliged if you would demonstrate that new turning technique we developed." The minister turned. " These gentlemen . . . Geordie, this is Mr. Harley and Mr. Rawlins—Geordie

MacTaggart." The minister was still bobbing up and down with excitement.

Geordie wiped the chicken mash off his hand and said how d'you do and fine, thanks, but he said it cool as he was very much vexed with the Laird of Drumfechan and in no mood for politeness.

"Come, come!" said the Laird impatiently. He strode off towards Geordie's house, still muttering about harmless kestrels. He was stooped at the shoulders, and he looked quite like a harmless old bird of prey himself.

The minister followed; then Mr. Harley and Mr. Rawlins whoever they might be in their fancy suits. Geordie brought up the rear carrying his two buckets. The atmosphere of the procession was very strained, what with the front and rear being angry and the minister in a state of high excitement, and the two strange gentlemen perhaps a little embarrassed at being the spectators of an ideological argument.

Geordie fetched the shot. He didn't want to give any demonstrations, but he couldn't very well refuse on account of the minister having been so good to him in different ways. He scored out a rough circle on the grass with his heel.

"Right," he said, avoiding the Laird's eye, and

the Laird avoiding his. There was much animosity between them. " Full strength, Mr. MacNab? "

" Full strength, Geordie," said Reverend MacNab.

Geordie took his stance, made himself comfortable, and putted the shot away with all the vexation he was still feeling. It was a beauty.

" Good God Almighty," said Mr. Harley.

" Well, I'll be ——" said Mr. Rawlins, forgetting the minister's cloth.

" Bravo," said the Laird without much enthusiasm.

" Not bad, Geordie," said Mr. MacNab. Even old Bess barked twice from the kennel.

Mr. Harley paced out the distance from the circle to the shot-mark. Then he walked over to Mr. Rawlins, ignoring the Laird and Geordie and the Reverend altogether.

" Forty-nine," he said. " It's fantastic in those heavy boots."

" It's bloody well colossal," said Mr. Rawlins. The minister coughed. " Sorry, Padre," Mr. Rawlins said. The two gents whispered together for another minute.

" No possible doubt," said Harley.

" None at all," Rawlins said.

They came over to Geordie. " Mr. MacTaggart," they both said, "we'd better explain who we are."

"Ughhugh?" said Geordie noncommittally. The Laird's conduct was still rankling with him.

"We are selectors for the British Olympic Games team."

"Is tha' a faact?" said Geordie.

"You know the Olympic Games are being held this summer?"

"I didna' ken," Geordie said. As a matter of fact he didn't ken rightly what like things the Olympic Games were.

The two gentlemen exchanged glances. They began to look a trifle uncomfortable as well they might in face of Geordie's vast and grumpy stolidity.

Mr. MacNab came to the rescue. "It's the World Athletics Championships, Geordie. They're to be held in America."

"In Amerriky, is it?"

Mr. Harley sighed. "We're inviting you to train for the Olympic Team."

Geordie grunted.

"They heard tell about you winning at Drumfechan last August," said Reverend MacNab. "Somebody sent a clipping from the *Herald and Journal.*"

" We want you to come to England for a month's training first," said Rawlins. " Then we sail for America early in July."

" I canna' spare the time."

The others looked uneasily at the Laird. His face was its usual healthy colour again. " We'll just have to spare you, George," he said.

" Putting the Shot for England! " said Mr. Harley reverently. " It's a great opportunity."

" What for would I put the Shot for England? "

" He means Britain," said Mr. Rawlins. He scowled at Mr. Harley.

" I'm ower busy," said Geordie. " I've ma chickens. Then there's the grouse butts to mend, and the vermin to kill. The season'll be round again afore we know where we are. Besides, I don't like the notion."

Mr. Harley began to speak, but Rawlins stopped him with a hoarse whisper. Fortunately Geordie didn't hear what he said. " Shut up, Tom! Let them persuade him. There's no good arguing with these bare-somethinged savages."

" You'd better go, George," said the Laird, who by this time had forgotten about their argument. " Your Uncle Jim could do your work temporarily. He knows about chickens, too."

Uncle Jim was only a rabbit-trapper, and Geordie

didn't have much of an opinion of him. "My Uncle Jim'd sort the Laird's kestrels," he said to the world at large.

"No, by God he wouldn't!" said the Laird hotly.

So feeling ran high between them again, and it required all Reverend MacNab's tact to make the peace. In the end the minister persuaded Geordie to go to the Olympic Games, but he flatly refused to be trained in England.

"Reverend MacNab's a braw trainer," he said, and that was that.

Later on Messrs. Harley and Rawlins got into their car. They had been depressed after their interview with Geordie, but the Laird's whisky was now coursing warmly through their veins.

"I don't understand them," said Mr. Harley.

"Nor do I, thank God," said Mr. Rawlins.

They both laughed heartily. It was very pleasant driving through the valley, and the car was like a corner of some foreign field that was for ever England.

"If you ask me, Bill," said Harley. "We've bitten off a bit more than we can chew with this chap MacTaggart."

"Is tha' a Faact?" said Rawlins.

The sound of their merriment spread and moved

with them. A roe deer raised his head at the sound; and a late shepherd wondered what those two chaps in the car were laughing so heartily about.

* 8 *

GEORDIE leaned his bike against the grey stone wall of the Manse, and went up the steps to ring the bell. The minister came to the door himself.

"Come in, Geordie," he said, beaming. "Come in. I was just thinking about you."

They went into the minister's study. It was a small room, dark because of all the books that covered the walls. You would know from the titles that it was a minister's room, from that and from the big Bible which had a table to itself. But there were some photos too, groups they were, taken when Reverend MacNab had been at the college; and they helped to brighten the place up. The minister didn't look much different now except that he was balder on top and a bit more pudgy round the middle. He wore the same big grin that had a cheering effect on the folk he met. They sat down in the two chairs, Geordie on the edge of his.

" When are you away, Geordie? "

" The morn's morn in McCrimmon's bus. Syne I'm to catch the Night Scot for England."

" Are the spikes fitting comfortable now? "

Mr. Rawlins had sent Geordie a pair of spiked shoes. He said he ought to get used to them because everybody would be wearing spikes in the Olympics and they were a help anyway.

" The spikes is fine."

" Now, remember, Geordie . . ." and Mr. MacNab went on to give Geordie some last minute tips—how he wasn't to practise too hard on account of straining his arm, how he might need shorter spikes on the hard American ground, and how he shouldn't let the trainers alter his style much because there wouldn't be time for that.

" Do you think you'll be nervous, Geordie? "

" Yes, I doubt I'll be nerrvous." Sometimes at nights Geordie would get thinking about going to the strange places among the strange people, and great crowds there would be most likely. It made him nervous just turning it over in his mind.

" Well, if you get nervous, try thinking of home. Think of the glen, or a bit of the hill that's your favourite; or just think of Jean. That could be a help, Geordie."

Geordie looked up at Reverend MacNab. In

that quiet room everything seemed as if it would be all right; and it wasn't a cause for shyness that you loved a dark-haired lassie who lived nearby. The minister's face was serious for once; just a hint of a smile at the corners of his mouth where the deep creases were unexpected in his chubby face.

" I'll do that," Geordie said.

Reverend MacNab leaned forward. Suddenly he looked a little nervous himself. " You may meet temptation, Geordie. You may find people will make a fuss of you; and worldly women take a fancy to a fine simple laddie. Well, don't heed them; just you stay simple."

" I'm ower thick in the head for to get spoilt," said Geordie, speaking broad. He and the minister laughed.

" We'll say a short prayer," said Mr. MacNab. They stood up then, and Geordie closed his eyes, listening to the minister's prayer. He didn't ask God for Geordie to win the Olympic Games which was what Geordie had expected he would ask. He just prayed for strength and good guidance and a safe return.

" Aimen," said the Minister.

" Aimen," said Geordie.

He got on his bike and rode the three miles home. It was one of those rare days in the summer-time when a full wild wind blows from the west. It pushed him along now, up the winding slope of the valley road, and speeded him down the other side. It was all about him, blustering in his ears, sighing in the tall larches, bending the heavy-laden branches of the oaks and elms, rippling across the green fields of oats beyond the river. The whole earth was swept by the voice of wind, warm and alive. It was a great day for the last day before a journey. And as he rode along, he watched the white clouds racing by the tree tops, hurrying on their own careless journey.

Geordie was to meet Jean at eight. He was still early, so he walked slowly along the path towards the garden until he came to the dry stone dyke. That was the place where Jean had waited for him on a day long ago. The memory was clear in his mind. He had been small then, perhaps the smallest boy for his age in the whole county. Well, he was the biggest man now; but he didn't feel much different. It was queer that you would be the same person, big or small; that the thing inside you never changed, the something that was really you.

And Geordie remembered how Jean had climbed to the eagle's nest; and afterwards she had understood the feelings he was having that a lassie had done what he could not do. Perhaps that was the day he had first known Jean was the one for him.

He sat there for a while, letting his mind run over the past, coming back to him stage by stage through the known things which had happened, and on to the unknown things which would begin to-morrow. It was then that he suddenly remembered Henry Samson's letter. It had been lying in his pocket since dinner-time, and never opened yet.

" Dear Geordie,

Thanks for favour of yours. Accept my hearty congrats on your great success. You may be sure that my eyes and ears will be glued to the newspapers and the wireless respectively, and that I for one will follow you on your triumphal way in the Olympics with bated breath.

It is a far cry from the day I received your first letter. I knew even then that you had the right stuff in you, Geordie; but I never guessed that you would turn out to be my finest pupil. It is a hard road to success, and you have travelled it. We can both be proud of what we have achieved together in the way of balanced development.

If the weather is favourable, I hope to be on

the quay at Southampton to make your acquaint-
ance at last, and to wish Bon Voyage, Au Revoir,
Happy Landings, the Best of Luck and God
Speed to a great pupil of Henry Samson's in the
Olympic Games.

Mens sana in corpore sano. You are the
living emblem of those immortal words.

Your old friend and admirer,

HENRY SAMSON "

That was certainly the best letter Henry Samson
had ever sent him. Geordie folded it up and put
it back in his pocket. To think of Mr Samson
perhaps coming to Southampton to see him off. It
was an honour you could bet he'd never given to any
other of his pupils.

But here was Jean. He watched her come walking, trying to make a vivid picture of her in his
mind that he could take away and keep with him in
America. But he was feared he wouldn't be able.
The faces you loved best never came into your
mind's eye. Or perhaps he would see her for a
second in the darkness and lose the picture.

She had on a blue dress this evening, quite short,
so that Geordie was able to watch the supple
slimness of her legs; and he saw the way her hair
flew in the high wind.

He put out his two big hands and took hers and helped her to a seat on the wall beside him, and his arm was round her waist and they sat quiet and happy with the west wind on their faces. But the cloud of parting hung over them there in the sunlight.

" The birches are bonny," said Jean. They were truly bonny with the leaves dancing on slender twigs, and the dappled trunks. The hill birches were twisted trees, growing against the storms, most beautiful on days of tempest.

" It's you is bonny," Geordie said. He held her closer to him.

" Did you get packed up? "

" Yes," said Geordie. " I've just the one suit-case."

" And the Kilt? "

" That's in too."

Silence again.

" There's the eagle! " said Geordie suddenly. They watched the great bird sweep fast across the far hill and disappear; and that gave them a memory of the time when they were pals, before there had been any lively magic between them.

" Are you going to win? "

Geordie pondered over this; looking at the lashes downcast over Jean's eyes, seeing the small straight nose she had, and the pale softness of her neck below the dark hair.

" I dinna' ken," he said. " Maybe I'll win. Och yes, I'll win." Perhaps he felt a wave of that self-confidence which accompanies most Scotsmen on their travels.

" Don't be too confident," said Jean. " You've the world against you."

" Here," said Geordie. " Here's what Henry Samson says." He gave her the letter. Jean read it through.

" Well, that's nice," she said, and gave it back to him without saying anything more.

" Are you not pleased at what Mr. Samson says? " Geordie felt a bit hurt that Jean should make no comment about the letter.

Jean frowned. " I like it fine," she said, " but I'm feared you'll get a swelled heid in among all the fancy folk."

" Och away," said Geordie. " You and Reverend MacNab's a pair. I'm telling you both: I'll not get a swelled heid."

She leaned right close and looked up at him. " Jest come back to me, Geordie. That's all I'm caring."

" Dinna' fash yerself," said Geordie. " I'll come back to my wee Jean." And he bent and kissed her. They'd had some practice the last year, so their kisses were becoming expert. This one went on for a long time, and the warm clean wind touching their cheeks.

But Jean was still worried about something, for her face was troubled even after that long kiss.

" Geordie! "

" Ay, Jean? "

" You'll no get mixed up with any other lassies? Them Yanks is terrible taken up wi' love. That's what I hear tell."

" What for would I take up wi' other lassies when I've my own Jean waiting? "

But the two tears rolled down her cheeks.

" Dinna' be sad, my bonny Jean. It'll no be long."

" I'm not sad," she said with a gulp. " I'm greetin' for happiness."

Geordie had never known Jean like this before, her with a mind so much quicker than his, and often a bit sharp with him. But now she had given herself into his hands; and it was a sweet thing for him to feel.

What was it Rabbie Burns had said, Rabbie who knew the song of love?

" Listen, Jean," he said.

" O my Luve is like a red red rose
    That's newly sprung in June:
    O my luve is like the melodie
    That's sweetly played in tune! "

He couldn't remember the rest of the verses, but
he knew about them. " Yon was a song at parting,"
said Geordie. " Yon was a promise to be true."

So Geordie and Jean sat a while longer, till the
great wind died at sunset and the brightness faded
from the bell heather.

* 9 *

GEORDIE stood at the rail, looking down on England. He'd only been a few hours in these southern parts, and here he was leaving already. The small neat fields, the brick houses, the harvest brown a month early, the crowds of folk, that station in London like a roofed world of its own it was so big, the rattle and the clatter and the hollow echoes of the train at night, and now the ship. It was all too much to take in at once. You got so filled up with strange things that you hardly noticed them any more.

The last rope had splashed into the water, the last deep blast had sounded from the ship's foghorn and made Geordie jump up there on the boat deck although he was not a nervous chap by any means, and there was a tiny tremor ran through his feet from the timbers of the big ship, and she began to move ahead inch by inch, and yard by yard.

But Geordie was not interesting himself at that moment in the sailing of the ship. He was looking down at the quay where a great specimen of manhood stood alone.

Henry Samson wore a green suit. It was as green as a field of young wheat; and even if he had been a small and insignificant man he would have shone like a beacon among the ordinary mortals on the quayside. But Henry Samson was neither small nor insignificant. He was a colossal man who had entirely come up to Geordie's expectations.

Now he stood a little apart from the other people, hands in the jacket pockets of his bright suit, legs apart, a wide-brimmed hat cocked jauntily on his head. He had eyes only for Geordie MacTaggart. There was something beautiful in the sight of those two vast men joined in physical communion across the widening space between ship and land.

When Geordie had got off the boat-train, he had kept a watch for Mr. Samson. It was a fine morning, so the chance of him coming should be good; and sure enough, there was a man along the dock who could have been no one but him. Their eyes met above the heads of the crowd. Mr. Samson swept off his wide hat with a flourish; Geordie raised his cap; and regardless of the small people about them, they strode to a meeting.

Geordie was shy, not knowing how he would support a conversation with a stranger yet a man he knew well through correspondence. But he need not have worried, for Henry Samson took charge of the situation.

" Geordie MacTaggart! " he shouted when he was still some distance off. All the heads turned.

" How do, Geordie? How are you, sonny? We've waited long for this."

" I'm fine," said Geordie.

They shook hands. Geordie took in Mr. Samson. He wasn't quite as tall as Geordie himself, but he was broader, and you could see from every line of his body that he was in fine shape, even although he must have been old, nearly forty. He was such a splendid figure that you couldn't help being disappointed in a way that he had to wear a suit of clothes, and not just be in his tiger-skin drawers. That would have seemed more natural like, although of course it would hardly have been the thing on Southampton dock.

" This is a great occasion, Geordie." He felt Geordie's muscles all over with a craftsman's pride, with a clinical interest, and swept his hand in a commanding gesture. The people were silent and watchful.

" Here's Geordie MacTaggart," he called, and his voice drowned the hubbub of quayside noises. " A braw laddie frae Bonny Scotland." Mr.

Samson's Scottish dialect was painful to hear. " He started from small beginnings, and look at him now. Look at his development! Isn't it splendid? He and I did it. We did it together."

By this time Henry Samson had drawn a large crowd about them. But he had not finished yet; there was a tremor of emotion in his voice as he went on:

" I am Henry Samson, and this is my finest pupil. This is Geordie MacTaggart, Olympic Shot-Putter, future World Champion. Wish him luck! "

The tears were rolling unashamedly down Mr. Samson's cheeks. Perhaps, like Mr. Churchill, he was easily moved by the sadness of great rejoicing.

There was a loud cheer then, for Mr. Samson and Geordie had captured the imagination of the people. " Good luck, Geordie! " shouted a stevedore.

Geordie felt confused, but so many queer things had been happening in the past twenty-four hours that he was not so surprised by Henry Samson's behaviour as he would have been if it had happened, say, up the glen at home. He thought perhaps that many Sassenachs were like Mr. Samson; in fact that he was nothing much out of the ordinary for an Englishman. But this was far from the truth, for Henry Samson was an extreme rarity in England, a most egregious character in that land of reticence, and the impact of his personality was startling wherever he went.

There had not been time for much talk; and Geordie himself had not spoken more than half a dozen words altogether. He hadn't had a chance.

Now he looked back towards the land. The green figure still stood on the quay, but inexorable distance had reduced even Mr. Samson to smallness. Geordie was thinking it was about time to go below.

Just then Henry Samson cupped his hands. " God bless you, Geordie! " The words of bene- diction sounded deep and clear across the water.

" Ta-ta, Mr. Samson," called Geordie. His was a loud hail too.

He went down to his cabin. Who should be sitting on the other bunk but that Mr. Rawlins who had come to Drumfechan to select Geordie for the Olympics.

" Hallo," he said cheerfully. " We're sharing a cabin."

This was no coincidence. "Look here, Bill," Mr. Harley had said. "You may not like the idea either, but someone will have to look after this MacTaggart chap; he's right out of the Highland jungle; and better you than me. I mean, you're more *en rapport*

with the Celtic temperament." So Mr. Rawlins
had given way, and being an amiable fellow, he
was going to make the best of what he feared might
be a bad job.

"Fine day," said Geordie. "How're you
keeping?"

"Passable, thank you," said Rawlins.

Geordie sat down on his bunk and wiped his
forehead which was damp because of all the strain
and excitement. "I'm fair bewildered," he said.

"Is this your first crossing?"

"It's the first time I was ever out of Perthshire."
Geordie felt like talking; he felt he had everything
bottled up inside and he had to get it out. So he
and Rawlins chatted for a while, and the latter
thought he must have formed the wrong impression
of Geordie on first acquaintance.

Then the tremble of the ship got bigger, and she
began to creak. It was a queer noise, not like anything he'd heard before; and the ship rolled slowly
with the creaking, and the porthole showed the
sea and then the sky and back again. It was a long
creaking, going a long way up from far behind,
that was the feeling you had about it.

"We're outside," said Rawlins. "I hear it's
going to be quite rough, so I hope you're a good
sailor."

H

Geordie was just going to tell him that he'd been on the loch often on rough days and never been sick at all, when there was a knock on the door and the cabin steward came in.   He was a pale-faced wee chap.

"Can I help unpack your bags, sir?" he asked.

"Who me?" said Geordie.   "Och, no thanks. I've just the one suitcase."

After the steward had gone out again, Geordie laughed and laughed.   He had an infectious laugh, so Rawlins began too.   "What's up?" he asked.

"It's that wee chap callin' me Sir," said Geordie. "And me never away from home till yesterday, and just with the plus four suit I've got on.   Who does he think I am, Andrew Carnegie?"

"They always call you Sir," said Rawlins.   He had taken a strong liking to Geordie already. "Come on!   Let's go up on deck."

It was three days before the sea was calm again. Geordie had not been right sick, but he had been squeamish and not able to do justice to the rare food that was provided.   Now the ship sailed ahead serenely, and the sunlit boat-deck was crowded with young athletes taking exercise—men and girls, tall and small, chunky and slim.   There were sombre springy Finns breathing sea air into their marathon lungs, gay Frenchmen and sad Frenchmen, blonde Nordics with skins tanned to the colour of ripe wheat, detached Englishmen, stolid Dutch, a couple of Lowland Scots, but not a single boy from the Highlands except Geordie.

They had one thing in common all these young people, a concern with the ultimate perfection of their specialised bodies; every step they took around the deck was taken with purpose, placed with design, executed with economy. This air of dedication lay deadly serious behind the most cheerful face. Geordie himself had been infected by it.

He stood now at the rail watching the shimmer of the water, thinking that a smooth sea was an endless thing, wishing that Jean could be with him to share the strangeness, feeling a bit lonely. And he listened idly to the people walking behind him, to the sounds of foreign speech, and sometimes an English voice; and all the voices he understood were talking of athletics.

" Hallo, Geordie."

" Hallo," said Geordie. It was Bill Rawlins.

" Want to come and have some practice? I got them to rig up a place on the well deck."

" I don't mind," Geordie said, and he and Rawlins made their way forward.

There were ten or twelve other shot-putters standing round a rig of deep coconut matting and strong nets to prevent the shot striking the boards of the deck. The chief officer was there too, him with the three stripes on his arm and a worried expression. " Please be careful of my deck," he kept saying, " Prenez garde "; and he was obviously on tenterhooks about the whole affair, because of course even a light practice shot could play havoc if it landed full pitch on the bare deck.

" He's a bit of an old mother," said Bill Rawlins. " I had the greatest difficulty in persuading him."

Geordie took off his jacket and rolled up his shirt sleeves. He had his rubber-soled shoes on. Most of the others were wearing grey trousers and proper athletics vests.

He waited his turn; and when it came, he took an easy one, just to get the feel of it again. The shot went well for him, thudding down on the matting and bouncing into the net. He fetched it back for the next performer.

But it was a girl who stepped forward to the line where Geordie was standing. He hadn't noticed her before; indeed he hadn't expected a lassie to be playing that game. Perhaps that was why he hadn't seen her.

"Hallo," she said, smiling at him from quite close. Then she bent, supple and quick, and stood again with the smaller ladies' shot in her strong hand. She had fair hair, just about the colour of pale gold, and it was tied up in a red ribbon behind her bare brown shoulders. She was wearing a vest like the men; it showed up the top half of her figure to perfection, almost too well in fact. What with that and the look of lively interest that she gave him and seeing such a big lovely woman unexpected, Geordie blushed scarlet. He dropped the men's shot with a bit of a bump on the chief officer's deck.

"It's all right, Geordie," whispered Bill Rawlins. "She won't eat you."

The girl took her practice. She didn't send it as far as the men, but she had a beautiful style, and it was obvious that she knew just as much about shot-putting as anyone.

"She's Scandinavian champion," said Bill while she was fetching the shot.

"Hallo, Beell," she said, seeming to know him quite well.

"Helga," he said. "This is Geordie MacTaggart from Scotland—Helga Sorensen."

"How do you do?" she said, shaking hands with Geordie.

"I'm fine," said Geordie. She certainly was a braw lassie, and if it hadn't been for the big scale she was constructed on, and the size of her shoulders, you would never have guessed her ability to put the shot.

"Do you live in the Scottish Highlands?" She spoke with a soft lilt. It gave a kind of a caress to the speech, like the way the people from the islands talked, the ones who had the Gaelic for their first language.

"Yes," said Geordie, looking down at her tanned face; but it was not far below his.

She smiled. "I thought," she said. "You are like the Highlanders. Ah, that is a most beautiful country. What you say? A bonny country. I was there one time, and I shall never forget it, neverr."

"Ay, it's bonny." She was so friendly and natural that Geordie felt less shy of her now.

While they waited their turn she told him in a low voice about the other shot-putters. "That is Weber, first string for Germany. He is very good, but a not nice man . . . Van Roon, champion of

Holland; but he is not quite big enough to win."
And so on. She seemed to know them all.

It was after they had had several practice shots,
and the gong had sounded for lunch and Geordie
felt very hungry, that she said: "They are all
good, these ones; but you, to me it seems you are
the, the dark horse. I think you will win."

Geordie was pleased at her saying that. It was
what he had been thinking himself. Seeing the
others at practice had made him keener than ever
before; and being so far away from home, he had
the feeling that it wasn't just Geordie MacTaggart
trying to win; it was Scotland that was in him, and
he would do his best and go back to Jean knowing
that.

"I wouldn't be surprised," he said. He had
never learned modesty. Modesty is a pleasant
thing; but the lack of it can be pleasant too in
plain people.

"We shall meet often and often, Geordie?"
She was looking seriously at him.

Geordie couldn't help feeling drawn to her, and
her being sympathetic at a time when everything
was new to him. But there was a wee murmur
in his mind, a murmur in Jean's voice which came
all the way across the ocean.

"Och, yes," he said.

Geordie and Helga did meet often. The next time they met was that evening. After his supper —dinner they called it for some reason—he went up to get a breath of fresh air on the boat deck. It was dark there; only a few people were about. He walked round several times, feeling the light breeze on his face, seeing the golden path which the moon made across the water, hearing the noises down below, the gentle strumming in the rigging; and the ship's bell sounded once from far away. It was a thing he couldn't explain to himself, but he felt that the ship and the sea were alive and he was a part of them, almost as much as he was a part of the living hill at home. He was thinking of Jean, of the letter he had written to her to-day, wondering if she had him in her mind too. So his thoughts were far away as he stopped walking to watch a light which came and went across the water.

He never heard her footsteps. " Hallo, Geordie," said Helga. " What are you doing? " She was wearing a long dress made of some stuff that caught the reflections; her arms and shoulders were bare, as they had been that morning.

" I was just thinking," he said. He rather wished she hadn't come up, even if he did like her friendliness.

" About what? "

" About home. I was thinking of Jean as a matter of fact." He said that right out.

" Of Jean? She is a girl then. She is the lucky girl? "

" I'm the lucky one," said Geordie.

" Tell me about this Jean."

So Geordie tried to tell her about Jean. He didn't make much of a job of the telling, but it was a thing he couldn't have brought himself to tell at all four days ago, so he wasn't doing so badly in his progress in the world.

" But she *is* lucky," Helga said, leaning a tiny bit closer to Geordie at the rail, so that her bare shoulder touched his. He wanted to move away; but he didn't bring himself to do it. It was too good being there in the moonlight with one person, and that an understanding lassie.

" She is lucky because you are a fine boy, so simple and kind."

" I'm like anybody else," said Geordie; he knew he was; still, he liked to have compliments paid him.

" Ach no," said Helga deep in her throat. " These others, you do not know them. Either they are stupid lumps, or they are . . . smart Alecs. And always they make paws at me. But you are different, Geordie. Already I know that."

If Geordie had been even a little more worldly-wise he would have scented danger then, for he was true to Jean in his heart. But he did not think of danger. He stood beside Helga in silence, glad of her company in the moonlit evening, watching the first light of America.

* IO *

THE next two days were like never getting off the whirly-birly with the wooden horses swinging round at a fair. That was how it felt to Geordie in New York. Skyscrapers, subways, room and bath, a zoo, and looking down from high up at the ship he'd just arrived in; it was all new to him. And when a chap said the Empire State was 1250 feet high, which was 100 more than the hill above Geordie's own house, you could have knocked him down with a feather.

So it was a rest for him to be sitting beside Bill Rawlins in the glittering Greyhound bus. He had the seat adjusted to the most comfortable position for his large frame, and he looked out of the window as they sped along the Merritt Parkway, special permission having been given for the buses to use it on the way to Boston.

Bill Rawlins was giving him a talk about America; and since it was an all-British bus-load except for the driver who was too far away to hear, he was able to express his opinions freely.

" Now take this parkway," he said. " It's a super road, isn't it? Enormous, superbly smooth, wider than anything you ever saw. In short, typically American."

" That's so," said Geordie.

" And here's another thing. You've seen their magazines? "

Geordie nodded. Of course he'd seen the mags. He'd been looking at the adverts every spare minute since arrival in the U.S.A.

" Well, the whole country is deluged with advertisement, super, hyper, duper. The cars have jet-flow aeroports, the sofas are feather beds with husband and wife facing outwards, the sheets help provide gracious living. Dammit, the oranges even have navels. Everything's perfect and it gets you down and there are so many vulgar blandishments you don't know where the hell you are.

" Now, here's the point. There isn't a single advertisement along this road, not one. The whole thing's in excellent taste. Look at the landscaping. Look at the grass and the trees, gentle curves, plain functional bridges. Now, isn't that remarkable? How did they resist the advertisers? Think how many there would be in England! I tell you, Geordie, it's an amazing country. You understand America perfectly at the first look. After you've

looked four times you don't know a damned thing."
He paused for breath.   It was one of his favourite
subjects.

" What for would you be trying to understand
it? " said Geordie.   " It's no yer ain hame.   Folk
seem different because of being in different places,
but they're folk just the same."

" Yes, yes, Geordie.   Perhaps you're right."
Bill sighed, for like most visitors he was anxious
to resolve the enigmas of the United States.

The bus rolled on through New England.
Geordie liked the gentle rolling country, so different from his own home; and he liked the white
houses, although it was hard to understand how
folk could live behind wooden boards an inch thick
with the wind blowing through most probably.

Two hundred miles is a long way even in the
most comfortable bus, so Geordie was cramped by
the time they began to run into Boston.   Also he
was very hot in his thick plus fours.

" I'd like fine to get started practising again."

" You'll be able to practise to-morrow.   By the
way, Geordie, what about vests and shorts?   Have
you got any? "

" I've two vests," said Geordie, " but I'm not
keen on wearing the kilt just for practice.   Shorts
would be fine for that."

" Have you got a kilt with you? "

" Ay, it's in the suitcase." Geordie nodded to the rack above his head.

Rawlins looked surprised. " You're not thinking of wearing your kilt in the Games? "

" That's what I'm to do."

" But look here, Geordie; no one else will be wearing a kilt."

" Well, it was the last thing I promised mum. ' Right, Mum,' I says, ' I'll wear the kilt.' So I'll be wearing it."

" I don't think you *can* wear it," said Bill, hovering between laughter and dismay. " Anyway, you'd look a bit ridiculous, wouldn't you? I mean, America's hardly a kilt-wearing country."

" No, but Scotland is." Geordie was hot and tired, fed up with sitting in a confined space. He felt his hackles rising when Bill Rawlins said that about the kilt. He'd brought it all the way to America folded up neatly in his suitcase, and it was dad's kilt, and a good luck thing and he'd never win unless he had it on.

" Are you really serious, Geordie? " Bill Rawlins watched Geordie's red face. It was fixed in a sort of expressionless obstinacy which Bill remembered from their first meeting in Scotland. Geordie was serious all right.

" Well, I'll ask the committee, but I don't think they'll agree. They want everyone to be dressed alike."

" I canna' help it," said Geordie. " No kilt, no performance. You can tell them that." He looked out of the window at the traffic crowding helter-skelter into Boston.

Geordie dried himself after the shower and went back to his room. He'd had a good final practice —some loosening exercises of Henry Samson's, and a few wee puts to keep his arm in tune. Now he felt just right for the great day of the finals to-morrow. It would have been a pity if he hadn't been able to perform after coming so far, but the committee had given way in the end about the kilt. It had been a battle, though.

Rawlins had tried to persuade him again. " Look here, Geordie. It can't make any difference whether you wear a kilt or not. In fact you'll do better in shorts; the thing's so damned heavy."

" I've said all I'm to say," said Geordie.

Then Harley: " It's not fair on the rest of the team. Besides you'd look conspicuous."

To which Geordie made no reply.

Finally Lord Paunceton who was head of the

committee: " After all, MacTaggart, it's a British team, not one from Scotland."

" I canna' help it, Your Lordship," said Geordie, who knew fine how to speak to Lords on account of meeting them often at Drumfechan. " I didn't want to come to America, but I was persuaded. My mind's made up."

" Why is he so damned obstinate about it ? " said Paunceton afterwards. " He seems a nice feller."

" He's a damned obstinate character," said Rawlins. " But there must be some reason apart from his mother wanting him to wear it."

" How much do we need him ? "

" He may turn out to be a flop, but I believe he's our only hope. That padre chap who trained him in Scotland wrote to me a fortnight ago. He said . . ." Rawlins looked around to see if any rival nations were in the offing, and lowered his voice to a whisper.

" What, really! Well, I suppose we'd better give way in that case. I don't like it, though. Pyjamas'll be the next national dress."

So Geordie was given permission to perform in dad's Black Watch kilt.

He got dressed again now and sat down to write to Jean. He'd written the once from the ship, so this was only the second letter.

Olympic Village

Boston

" Dear Jean,

We got here safe last Thursday in a bus all the road from New York. They have the engine at the back so you don't hear any noise except from the one in front if there is one. To-morrow is Putting the Weight. I am feeling great. First they didn't agree for me to wear the kilt, but I said, ' No kilt—No performance,' so they gave way in the end.

America is a big enough place and the Yanks seems decent folk for all the chew chew chew and the ties they wear you could see a mile off.

That Miss Helga Sorensen I was telling you about said would I take her with me for to see the town of Boston so am expecting her any minute now. She doesn't feel comfortable with the chaps in her team, which is why she asked me.

Well, Jean, I will close, hoping this finds you as it leaves me in the pink but missing Jean Donaldson.

Yours truly,

Geordie MacTaggart

P.S.—XX   S.W.A.K."

I

He'd just stuck on the American stamp when Helga arrived. She looked as large as life in a striped dress, red and white, and she gave Geordie her usual friendly smile.

" Hallo, Geordie," she said. " To-morrow is our big day, no? "

" Yes," said Geordie. Helga's noes and yesses got him fair mixed up.

They walked between the neat rows of huts which made up Olympic Village, under the archway at the entrance where the flags of every country drooped in the hot July afternoon. Outside, the cars went by in a chromium-plated stream; you watched them and wondered how so many people could each have a car to himself, and all the same facing both ways, shining new, and yet a little different, like eggs would be different from the same hen; and every now and then a square old car you would feel had a character of its own; and the lorries bearing the names of places far away, blowing a gust of exhaust and a tremble at you as they thundered by.

It was frightening. It drew Helga and Geordie into a small circle of their own strangeness.

The bus came along soon. They climbed in, paid the driver and took their seats at the back.

Helga leaned her shoulder against his, like she'd

done that evening on the ship. "Are you nervous for to-morrow?"

Geordie was nervous. It was just beginning to come at him now in the bus in among the traffic —the thought of standing out alone in that huge stadium before all the crowds, and him in the kilt he had to wear for dad's sake and different from everybody else.

"Ay, I'm nervous."

"Geordie, you should not be. You will win. I know you will win."

"I don't think it."

"You *must* win. You must beat that . . . that Weber. I shall wish with all my heart. I shall bite my teeth for you to win."

"What about your own Norway chap?" said Geordie. "Do ye no want him to win?"

Helga hung her head, and a slow blush spread over her tanned face and round behind her neck. It was very becoming. For the first time Geordie felt a tingle in him when he looked at Helga; it was not plain friendship for the girl who put the shot like he did; it was something different, something which said: I am unknown and desirable. Come and find me out.

"I should . . ." she murmured. "I know I should. But I cannot, Geordie. It is you I want to

win." She raised her big blue eyes and looked
sadly at him.

Just then the bus stopped where Boylston Street
comes to the Public Garden, and Geordie and
Helga hurried to get off in time. Then they had
to watch out for themselves crossing the street.
That made Geordie forget the queer feeling he had
just had about Helga.

They walked through the Public Garden, past
the foreign-looking flowers and the boats with big
swans at the back, under the elm trees where the
grass was very green. The Garden was crowded
with people wandering in the shade and in the sunlight—lonely people and happy people, family par-
ties and lovers, thin suits and thick, open necks and
bright ties, light people and dark, people from the
South and the Middle West and the Never-Never
land of sunshine; New Yorkers, plain men from
Maine, and all come to see the Olympic Games.
They walked slowly these people, but their eyes
were quick. They were on the look-out, that was
the feeling you had. They were watching for
something round the corner, something different,
something still newer than the things they had
already.

Beyond the trees and up the hill and down there
below the tall buildings the traffic rumbled and

muttered and whined in gathering speed, and the pigeons flew together. And it was Boston, a little aloof from all the goings-on.

Geordie and Helga walked farther. They talked of this and that, but it was a meaningless conversation for they were both self-conscious, very much aware of the attention they were receiving. America is a land of big people, but Geordie and Helga were a spectacular pair, and there was that thing about them which said that they were strange—not tall strangers from Kansas or from Arkansas, but strangers from a different place. And even if there had not been that stamp of difference, hard to understand, hard to define, Geordie's knickerbocker suit was an unusual garment on a July day in the green parks of Boston. So people looked and smiled and turned admiringly. Not that there was any rudeness in the interest, for Americans are kindly people who live a long way from one another.

"Let us see the shops," said Helga when they came near to the street which runs past a small old church and a steep narrow street beyond the Common. So they crossed Tremont beside the subway and looked into the shop windows.

They felt less conspicuous there, because the people were hurrying to business or from business, on this errand or that, and they had less time to be interested in a couple of young giants who had come to Boston from the Old World.

Helga kept him waiting a good long time outside a hat shop while she scanned the windows. He watched the folk passing for a bit; then he watched the cars; finally for want of anything better to do he began to watch the hats. The idea came to him all of a sudden. Ever since he'd arrived in America he'd been wanting to get a present for Jean, but there hadn't been much time for shopping, and the few things he'd thought of wouldn't do on second thoughts. Not any hat, but that one there: that one there made of green straw stuff with rows and rows of grapes all round it and a red feather and a veil hanging down the front. It was just the thing Jean would like fine to wear to the Kirk on Sundays. It was a beauty of a hat.

"Helga," he called. She was further along the big window. She came dutifully. "See yon hat!"

Helga's eyes brightened for a second. Was he going to give her a hat? But Geordie disillusioned her at once. "I was thinkin' mebbe I'd get it for Jean."

"You mean the hat with so many fruits?"

Geordie nodded. The tag said $7.95.

" But are you sure? Would such a hat suit Jean ? "

" Och yes. Yon's a braw hat."

Helga shrugged her wide and graceful shoulders. She was a nice girl, but there were limits. Who was she to stop him giving a dreadful hat to that girl in Scotland?

" I'll just get it," said Geordie. He strode bravely into the strange environment of a ladies' hat shop in Boston, and bought the hat from a middle-aged sales lady whose heart fluttered agreeably at the sight of him.

Geordie and Helga walked on down the street. He carried the big hat-box under his arm. It was five o'clock, that time of a summer's day when a whisper of coolness comes into the city and goes and comes again.

They were waiting to cross the road when it happened. Geordie chanced to be looking across the street. He saw a man, youngish and pale, step off the pavement, glance up to his left and hurry on. It was queer that he wouldn't have seen the car bearing down on him, a shabby black car, higher than the new ones. Perhaps the chap had one of those moments when a man's eyes don't tell him, perhaps he was distraught; he looked that kind.

Whatever it was, he was nearly in front of it

when the driver saw him coming out, and swung
the car across the road, going too fast to stop. But
the way he swung was the way the man was going
and it was too late when the chap on foot began to
check, and a blankness ironed out his expression
and he dithered still going across, the car doing
its best to go beyond him. There was nothing the
big van coming the other way could do about it
except try to stop, but it was moving fast too.
Brakes screeched, one horn sounded for a second
before the car and the van clashed into one another.
The van was tall and heavy. It tipped the car
neatly over on its side and on to its back. There
was a crunch of metal slithering to a stop and the
underneath of the car was tilted up there like some
mechanical nakedness and one of the front wheels
still turned slowly.

Geordie's feet were stuck to the pavement.
Silence came for a second before the hubbub of
people shouting, and a woman's scream, back of the
hand to her mouth, and a policeman running up
from nowhere, and Helga gripping Geordie's arm
tight.

He couldn't see what had happened to the man
on foot. He wasn't there any more, just disappeared. But the policeman was looking down
beyond the capsized car and the van driver went

round beside him; through the other noises Geordie heard the high sound which comes from a tortured man's throat, gets dragged out of him.

He shoved the hat-box into Helga's hand and ran out. He didn't have ten yards to go. The young man was lying on his back with the whole weight of the car bearing down on him. That noise was coming from him; the sweat was all over his twisted face. He wasn't nice to see. The policeman and the van driver were trying to lift the car, but they couldn't budge it. The car driver was still inside; but he didn't look hurt. He struggled with the door upside down.

" Here, I'll lift it," said Geordie. " One o' you pull him out." A thing he noticed in all that hurried moment was the stink of hot brakes.

He got his hands under the sharp corner of the roof, feet apart, trying to straighten his back; but it was heavy, it wouldn't come.

Geordie closed his eyes and heaved again, heaving against his held breath, against the strong pillars of his legs. He heaved until the darkness behind his eyes was a red hammering.

And the car came up. He only held it for a couple of seconds, but that was time enough. They pulled the chap out from underneath.

Geordie sat down to get his head straight. It

was the greatest physical effort he had ever made, but he was young and every muscle in his body was tuned for strength. He felt all right again soon, just a bit dizzy because of all the virtue that had gone out of him.

The injured man was quiet now. " Thanks, bud," he said weakly, looking at Geordie and managing a smile.

An ambulance arrived then and they loaded him in—a broken arm and a broken leg, compound it looked like; but he said his chest was O.K. Lucky enough to get off as light as that.

Geordie would have slipped away if it hadn't been for the young reporter who happened to see the crash. He came over in a hurry. It was a story; it might be a story. He'd been on the *Globe* six months, and he was mad keen.

" *The Globe*," he panted. " Dicky Martin from the *Boston Globe*. Did you lift that car alone? "

" I'll say he did," said the policeman with the Irish face. " He's a bloody Samson, that guy." He looked admiringly at Geordie; then went off to get the traffic moving past the upset car. Horns were sounding peremptorily all up and down the street. Another policeman arrived to get the details.

Geordie smiled to himself. That was a joke, the

bobby calling him a Samson, and him learning all his strength from Henry Samson.

Young Mr. Martin, who was about Geordie's own age, shepherded him over to the side-walk. He had his notebook out, and he was bubbling over inside with excitement but holding himself in iron control as a good reporter should. Helga had joined them; so they stood there, the three of them, big Geordie and big Helga, and small Dicky Martin as bright as a button.

" Say, who are you? "

" I'm Geordie MacTaggart."

" He's the famous shot-putter from Scotland," said Helga. " He is in the Olympics to-morrow."

Dicky Martin lost all his composure for a moment. " Oh gee, oh golly," he gasped. " This *is* a story. Geordie MacTaggart, did you say? Height six foot five. Weight? 20 stone. No, how many pounds? "

" I dinna' ken how mony pounds," said Geordie. He was flustered by Dicky Martin's high speed tactics.

" Highlander from lonely glen. Giant Caledonian saves life on eve of . . . Red hair. Didn't hurt yourself, did you? "

Geordie felt nearly all right again. He shook his head.

" How d'you like the States? "

" I like it fine," said Geordie. " The folk's decent, but it's ower hot."

That went down, and the other answers that Geordie gave, and certain embellishments which occurred to Mr. Martin's fertile imagination. He was a very bright cub reporter, slated for success.

He kept looking round uneasily for rivals. " I can get that injured guy's name later," he muttered to himself. " You're the scoop." He looked up at Geordie and Helga. " Come on! Let's get going." And he led them away from the danger of other reporters until he found what he was looking for—a photographer on the common who took a picture of Geordie and Helga standing beside Dicky Martin for a comparison of sizes.

" Will it be in the papers? " asked Geordie. Except for a brief passage in the *Herald and Journal* last year when he won at Drumfechan, and a few mentions a week ago in the New York papers, he had never seen his name, far less his picture in the Press.

" Sure it will," said Martin. " Look on the front page to-morrow morning. Thanks for everything. You're a swell guy. Well, good-bye." He shook hands warmly with them both and disappeared in a raging hurry.

" Oh Geordie, you are so wonderful," said Helga. She clung to his arm all the way back to Olympic Village in the bus; and Geordie never freed himself. That would be a lot to expect of a nice chap when a pretty girl says he's wonderful.

* II *

IT was a great load he was carrying. It was the weight of his sick dad, and he was coming off the hill, down the last steep bit into the valley where the smoke was sliced off flat from the cottage chimney. He slumped down beside the door. Mum would be coming in a minute, mum in a car that was upside down, mum in a braw hat with fruits. Here she was now.

Geordie opened his eyes. Bill Rawlins stood in the doorway of his room—not mum, a comfortable body with dismay in her eyes, but lean friendly Bill laughing all over his face and carrying a newspaper.

The dream slipped further back in Geordie's mind, and came a little and faded altogether; but the melancholy did not leave him at once. He sat up in bed feeling heavy after a good night's sleep ending in troubled dreams.

" Look at the front page! " said Bill. " All about some damned Scotsman called MacTaggart, some hero from away up the glen, oor Geordie."

Geordie was well accustomed by now to having his leg pulled by Bill; so he just took the paper, rubbed his eyes and began to read. The headlines stared him in the face.

" Kilt-wearing Caledonian's Feat of Strength on Eve of Olympics

" Geordie MacTaggart, copper-haired giant from away up the glen performed a remarkable feat late yesterday raising an upset auto unaided to free the victim of a Tremont pile up . . ."

It went on for a whole column, praising Geordie for taking the risk of a strain to his muscles, telling a lot of blether about his home which that chap must have made up because Geordie never told him the half of a fairy tale like that; ending up by saying that if an American couldn't win the shot-putting, then the *Boston Globe* hoped that modest Geordie would. The picture of him and Helga and wee Dicky Martin was in the middle of the page; it was a right good snap.

Geordie felt pleased as he read the story through; but after the second reading a kind of dismay began to creep over him. He gave the paper back to Bill.

" Don't you like it, Geordie? " said Bill, watching

him. "They always spread themselves about a thing like that."

"Och, it's all right," said Geordie. "It canna' be helpit. It's jest me in the kilt before all the folk, and me no wearin' it for the publicity's sake."

Bill said nothing.

"It was my dad's," Geordie said, looking over at the chair where the kilt was hanging to get the creases out. "He left it to me special, so I told mum I'd wear it. But I'm no wantin' to wear it for to be an exhibition. Maybe I'd better put on shorts." He looked very dismal.

"No, you'll have to wear it," said Bill gently. "You didn't ask for the publicity; and besides, I think your father would be proud of you." His voice changed. "Come on now, Geordie! Out of bed, you great lump!"

They were standing outside the entrance to the stadium, all the athletes dressed in white clothes, waiting group by group, nation by nation, talking and then silent again, the conversation rippling on and off along the line.

Geordie could feel the nervousness in himself, and he could hear the crowd beyond the high wall. He heard the distant babble and the high voice of a man selling something. But it was a feeling more than a hearing; it was the queer presence of a mass of people, and it bore heavily upon him.

The parade began to form up then behind the standard-bearers, a kaleidoscope straightening itself out from a jumble to a neat pattern. The British team had drawn last place in the procession, and because Geordie was dressed differently, they had asked him to march at the very back.

So he stood alone now, waiting for the doors to open up there in front, and the head of the procession to wheel into the arena where the people waited careless and comfortable with nothing to do but watch. In that uneasy moment Geordie thought of the crowd as an enemy, as a single lazy giant who could break him down with the force of its one eye, its many eyes that were one. And he saw suddenly how little his own bigness had ever done for him; how foolish he had been to waste many hours and years making his body strong. He understood for the first time why Jean had mocked him for his exercises. Had Henry Samson ever thought of that? Had he ever wondered if great strength really did return the penny?

The doors swung open. Geordie brushed the last piece of dust from his dark kilt, hitching it up so that it hung evenly all the way round. A band

K

was playing somewhere beyond that high wall. The front of the column began to move. The head of the elegant white snake swung through the doors. The whole column rippled from suspense to action, and the first sound of cheering came from the arena.

There is the way you see a diamond, the way your eyes narrow to its single lustre, all else excluded. There is the other way of looking, when you watch a range of hills, or the wide bay at sunset, and see the whole unbroken. This was how Geordie saw the crowd, not sharply, not as a multitude of single pieces, but in a wide brightness of colour and noise and movement within stillness.

He came through the door now, following the men ahead of him, hearing the waves of cheering flow and ebb, high voices and deep, and the noise a living thing in the sunlight. He felt very much alone, but no longer afraid of that Person of People which stretched up and up the tiers in the corner of his eye. His legs went easily to whatever tune the band was playing, a merry tune that said, Now LEFT FOOT, right foot, LEFT FOOT, right foot; and he swung his arms as dad had taught him long ago, chest square, chin in, with the turning swaying imperceptible emphasis of bottom, and the pleats of the kilt in rhythm. But something sharp came through the noisy air. It was a call for him. " Hi,

Geordie!" in a man's voice of strength, and the cheering doubled after that, and Geordie marched on alone at the tail of the column.

Jim Cameron was by himself in the unreserved seats where the sun was hot. He was from Wyoming, buying blood horses in the East. That's a likely make of a colt I bought yesterday, he thought. Can't wait to see him back home. Why did I come? What a goddam waste of a morning. Ah, here they are now.

He watched the stalwart German team, the springy Finns, the tall Americans marching with limber strides, telling a small proud tale of freedom to him and every other American. He watched the other nations pass, all of them, until there were only the British still to come. They moved freely too. Jim Cameron saw them briefly; then his eyes moved to the solitary kilted boy. He looked a lonely giant in his different clothes.

Jim watched him casually at first, with the measuring, dispassionate eye which breeders turn to any living thing. He remembered the story in the *Globe*; half-heard the people talk around him; half-heard the sigh of a pretty woman whose eyes were looking that way too.

" A husky-looking guy . . . Lifted an automobile
. . . Could be an American . . . Copper-haired giant,
that's what the *Globe* said. . . . Primitive, isn't he
. . . Swell the way his kilts swing."

" A man like that in a kilt does something to
me," said the pretty woman to her companion. Her
lips were parted and her eyes were shining. It very
evidently did do something to her. It did something to the college girl. It did something to the
older lady who remembered her own dead son and
wished she hadn't put on her new shoes.

It does something to me too, Jim thought. But
it does a different thing. Twenty-five years since
I came over; twenty years since I was a grown-up
American, twenty years since I forgot the feeling of
the seeing of the kilt. But I see the place again now.
I see Ben Slioch rising steep from Loch Maree. I
see something that I never saw back in Wyoming
in my home. I thought it left me long ago; but
it never went away.

The tears ran down Jim Cameron's cheeks, and
he was not ashamed. He filled his lungs of brass
and called to Geordie. He called for the bare-footed
days of his childhood, he called for Scotland, called
in the voice of America: " Hi, Geordie! "

Now the back of the column was swinging round the stadium, coming into the straight which lay below the covered stands. The cheering rose and fell as the people greeted each passing group, cordially with shouts, coolly with polite clapping. As was natural and right, the American team received the high ovation; but next after them the greatest shouts were for Geordie. It is a strange thing the capturing of human fancy—when a single man or a single woman will arouse warm ownership in a hundred thousand. And that was what Geordie did. The news story that morning, the handsome size of him, sombre and stolid yet light of foot, the unfamiliar dress he wore, his last place in the company of athletes; it must have been a harmony of all these things.

He knew it as he marched on to the changing tunes of every country. He knew that the people cheered for him. But Geordie was not there. He marched proudly for the sake of Scotland. His mind flickered from America to home and Jean. But he was in none of the places; he was with none of the people; he was not with himself. He was outside somewhere, outside the hubbub and the bright colours and the martial music.

Then the band changed to the English tune, the British Grenadiers, and Geordie came part of the way back from his day-dreaming. He saw the backs straighten in front and arms swing higher. They were coming to the place of salute where the President of the United States stood on a platform, grey hat held across his chest. There was a nobility about the single figure, head of the nation, clothed as an ordinary man, standing quite still below the battery of flags.

Geordie was still twenty paces from the President when the music changed again. They hadn't changed it in the practice yesterday. This was something unrehearsed.

The new tune sent a shiver up his back and down his legs and up again, hovering sweet and bitter in the hairs of his neck. It was Highland Laddie, not played with the tangle-jangle of the pipes, but Highland Laddie all the same, bearing its own message for him in a green arena in a foreign land.

The President looked straight at Geordie, tilted his chin, smiled a little. Then he was away behind, and the Eyes Front was given, and the Highland tune was company.

This time Geordie's thoughts did not hover betwixt and between, outside and in, under and over. He was ten years old, walking with his dad into the Queen's Barracks, into the grey parade ground in a grey part of a city. The pipes and drums were drawn up ready, and they began to play. It was a queer setting for the playing of Retreat. You would expect it to be on the green grass, or in the shadow of the hills, but not in a murky quadrangle below high chimneys. And yet it was a noble frame for the contrast of green doublets and scarlet, for the bright pipers' kilts and the dark kilts of the drummers, and the Drum Major twirling his silver stick in front, and the sound of pipes and drums filling the space between the buildings, the sound that made you feel hot and cold, happy and sad. Perhaps you got the message better in that dull place.

Geordie and his dad never spoke for the whole half-hour—march and counter march, forming circle, strathspey and quick reel-time, the slow lilt of Lochaber No More. But it was Highland Laddie that carried you away, took you on its wild flood and fixed the memory of that one evening so that you remembered it ten years later in Boston, Massachusetts, in the U.S.A.

There was more to remember too. There was a big voice sounding behind: " MacTaggart! " Dad gave a jump and turned round and stiffened up, bringing his heels together in a comical out-of-practice way. " Yessir," he said. The chap was dressed up like an officer, with a fancy belt, and he

had a wide moustache on him. He looked fierce
even when he smiled for a second at dad. And for
all his officer's get-up he spoke broad. " This your
laddie? "

" Yessir," said dad, still standing stiff even though
it was eight years since he finished his time in the
regiment. " Geordie's his name."

The big man took his glove off and shook hands
solemnly with Geordie, and went away, no words
spoken.

" Wha's yon, Dad? " asked Geordie.

" Yon's the great Charlie Scott," said dad.
" R.S.M. in my day, Q.M. now, and a right terror.
I'm scared o' him yet." Dad laughed. It was the
first time Geordie had ever heard of him being
scared of anything or anybody.

But swinging round the end of the track, coming
back now to the doors where they had entered the
arena, Geordie understood why his dad had gone
sometimes to see the kilt hanging in the cupboard;
why he had given it to him specially on the day
before he died.

The big doors closed off the noise behind him.
Geordie was outside again. The beginning of the
day was over.

∗ 12 ∗

GEORDIE sat on the grass in the centre of the arena. He was waiting. It was pleasant enough, for there was a breeze which fanned away the heat of the sun, kept him cool except at the waist where the kilt gripped him tight. It would be pleasant enough if it wasn't for the heaviness that was in him. He listened to the swarming murmur of the crowd, like bees they sounded now, but without purpose, not going for the nectar to make honey; just sitting there, watching a few folk doing daft capers for an entertainment.

"Last round commencing," said the man in white flannels at the microphone. His voice spread about and sounded back, sounding loudest from the covered stands. There were a few men standing on the high roof, policemen would they be, or firemen? The conversation faded. You saw a white movement of programmes all the way round.

But the announcer was speaking again: "Weber, Germany, leads with 52 feet 6. Second—Hendricks, U.S.A., 52 feet 3¼. Third—Van Roon, Nether-

153

lands, 51 feet 4½. Fourth—MacTaggart, Great
Britain, 51 feet 1 inch."

The first three men took their final turn. None
of them did better than fifty, so they were out of it.
But now it was Van Roon from Holland. He
jumped up lightly. He was a graceful fellow, more
like a sprinter than a shot-putter, but big of course.
They called him the Flying Dutchman. With the
smile on his face, and the careless way he had, you
always thought it was a game with him. But perhaps
it wasn't; perhaps he was icy cold and serious
underneath.

The shot landed with its soft pud, and measurements began again, judges solemn like it was a
funeral. " 51 feet 2 inches." A round of applause,
warm and friendly, saying bad luck you didn't win.
Van Roon was a favourite with the crowd. He
shrugged his shoulders once, up and down, mobile
and expressive, and smiled and came back to where
the others were sitting.

Geordie had time yet to wait, for he was last
man on the list. " Aye last," he muttered, looking
down at his bare legs stretched out in front, fuzzy
red hair all over them, ugly to see. Last in the
parade, last in the shot-putting. The last shall be
first, it said in the Bible; but that was a different
meaning.

Then Weber's name was called. He stood up deliberately, glanced as deliberately to the right where Helga Sorensen sat with the other girls, waiting to compete after the men's event. But Helga's eyes were on Geordie. He felt them on himself all the time.

There was no lightness about Weber, no smiles, no grace. He was a purposeful *Übermensch*; arrogant, and yet a little doubtful. You could see the chip he carried on his shoulder, the chip which said: " *Wir sind doch besser* "; *doch, doch, doch*, we are, we are, we are. And it was nearly true; it could have been true. So if you had the detachment of God you might feel sorry for him and for all the other Webers.

" Weber, Germany, 53 feet exactly." It was a magnificent put. He sat down, still sombre of face. " Good one," said Geordie. " Danke," said Weber, looking quite human for a moment, forgetting his *Schicksal*, his Germanic destiny, in a personal honest satisfaction. He's a decent enough chap, Geordie thought suddenly. But Geordie had had it easy in his glen. He couldn't understand the long story which put the melancholy prickles into Weber.

" Hendricks, U.S.A." The cheers of encouragement sounded from every direction.

" Geordie! " It was Helga there beside him.

She took his hand, and squeezed it, looking at him with the open adoration which stirred him and embarrassed him too. " Good luck, Geordie." She went away again.

Hendricks was at the circle. He had that impersonal dedicated look about him, utterly absorbed; and calm you would think. So he was calm, but the muscles tightened and loosened in his cheeks. That told you the electric charge that was inside him.

Geordie watched him in the hush, not seeing though. It was his own turn next. He began to rub his right arm up and down. The muscles were loose as they should be. But he wasn't right inside himself. Down there in his stomach he was knotted up tight, and in his head too. This was the last chance you came to, the moment you'd trained for; and you weren't right for it. You were a muckle lump of nerves, not even caring that there was no spark inside you.

Think of home, the minister had said. So now Geordie tried to think of home. He tried to carry his mind beyond the crowd of people, away beyond the loneliness of being shut in before the eyes. He tried to think of the skeery place where the eagles used to nest, but that was a place where eyes might watch you too. That was no good. He tried to

think of the grouse calling in the early morning when
the mist still lay about the moor. He could see the
mist eddying. It wasn't hidden mist he wanted.
It was a calm clear day of sunshine, him sitting on
a high top and seeing all the world below and no
one seeing him. But it would not come to help him.

Cheering again; not loud enough to mean a
winner. No, Hendricks hadn't done it. " Hendricks, U.S.A., 52 feet 8¼ inches." Cheers and
claps and calling and disappointment.

" MacTaggart, Great Britain." Now it was him
and he was on his feet. The roar of applause swept
round and above him. They wanted him to win;
he knew that for sure. They wouldn't be shouting
their heads off if they didn't wish him well. But it
was no good; he didn't have the power of extra
guts in his stomach; he didn't have the bright
purpose in his mind. They could shout and shout,
and it would do no good.

Young Dicky Martin of the *Boston Globe*, he was
the one who saw that captivating thing in Geordie;
he was the one who gave them the idea. Their
own man had failed to win, so now the Americans
took Geordie to their hearts. They shouted for
him, the ladies—motherly, sisterly and with a
different admiration. The ladies shouted heartily
for the kind of man you dream you may meet some

place by chance.   And the men because he looked
a nice guy, and strong as they would like to be, and
a kilted Scotsman;   hence a joke was in behind it,
and less controversial than if he had been English.
And the small boys and girls cheered because it was
infectious.   You must win now, Geordie, was what
they all were feeling.

He took the shot in his hand, and silence fell
again, such a silence as you could touch.   The
Hamburger men, the soft drinks men, the ice cream
men, they stood still.   It was that kind of a moment,
charged up with a single thought in many minds.

Jim Cameron waited till then to give his shout.
This time he shouted in the remembered words of
Scotland, in the great voice which would echo
in his mountainous Wyoming.

" Come away now, Geordie," bellowed Jim
Cameron, Highland boy and American.

Geordie heard that as he stepped into the circle.
He heard the familiar words.   They did not do the
trick;   they did not free him.   But they called up
something else.   It was the face of Jean.   He had
striven hard these last two weeks and never seen

her face. He saw her now, just as sharp and clear as if she was before him—grey eyes and smiling lips and hair unruly in the wind.

That was not all. In the hush he heard her speak to him. She sounded close out there where he was lonely. She gave the strength he could not find himself.

" Come away now, Geordie," she said in her soft urgent voice. " Come away, my wee Geordie."

It was like a snap the way it happened. The knots were untied in his stomach; the load jumped off his shoulders; the nervous misery had left him.

" Och ay, Jean," he murmured, facing the board, speaking so low that no one would hear except himself in his own ears; and mebbe Jean would hear.

Geordie MacTaggart did his put. There she goes, he thought, watching the ball spin slowly as it climbed. There she goes. I got rid of her that time. That's the last one. That's the last I'll ever do. Up and up and still for a moment at the peak. And down she starts to come, down across the white blobbed faces, faster faster like the Bible swine going helter-skelter for the brink. Bye-bye, Henry Samson.

The shot plunked dully. It lay far beyond the other marks.

"Aaah!" The long gasp of people who have no words to say. It shuddered round the stadium and died, and there was a silence before the storm of cheering.

Geordie dusted his hands on his kilt and walked out of the circle. He smiled for the pride of victory, for the lightness of his troubles over, for the pleasure of the pandemonium. People were running, vaulting the rail at the edge of the arena, coming to him from every direction, and the hats flew and programmes fluttered in the breeze.

He just caught that glimpse of people running to him, like the ripples of a stone reversing, like the chickens running for the mash.

But Helga reached him long before the others. She threw herself at Geordie, knocking him off balance so that he clutched to save himself. Her arms were round his neck. "Oh, Georrdie, oh, Georrdie. You are so wonderful." She clung to him and kissed him passionately.

First the shock of winning; then the shock of Helga's impact; the electric shock of her kiss, the soft delightful shock of clinching with a muckle lassie.

Helga stood proxy then; it was several seconds before Geordie thought of disengagement.

The wireless crackled; the American voice grew louder and faded and came again. But it wasn't bad reception for short wave.

" It's as good as I can get it," said Reverend MacNab, fingering the knobs with his red face close to the loudspeaker. Then he sat back in his chair; but he kept bouncing about in a restless way.

Jean sat still, just looking at the place the noise came from, the way people do. She could hear the steady drizzle of rain on the rhododendrons outside the minister's study window.

". . . That's a disappointment about Hendricks. He did splendidly, though. Now it's the last man of all. Now you people over there in Scotland, it's your own man, Geordie MacTaggart. I've been watching that boy all morning. It's wonderful to see the composure he has, sitting out there on the grass, not a worry, not a care. Ideal temperament. And when you think he's new to all this.

" Now he's standing up, going over to the circle. Listen to the cheering, listen to the way the crowd is wishing him luck. I can't tell you what it's like. That boy, that braw Highland Laddie, has won the heart of America. The people are mad for him. It's not only what he did yesterday . . ." The voice faded right out.

The minister tutted irritably. But it came back:

L

" Not since the great John L. Sullivan, the Boston Strong Boy, the idol of the people of this city—not since John L. Sullivan has Boston felt like this about a man. I venture to say that. Yes, I venture to say it. No diamond studded belt for Geordie perhaps, but our thoughts are with him, our fervent hopes and wishes.

" Now he has the shot in his hand. Silence now, absolute silence. You could hear a pin drop, yes literally; and the stands are still, literally absolutely still. He's stepping out to the circle, kilt swinging, the picture of confidence. There's something about that boy. We all feel he can win, but two feet's a lot of distance.

" Did you hear that shout? Just one man's tremendous voice. I don't know what he called. Now MacTaggart's in the circle. He's standing there, taking rather a long time."

Come away now, Geordie, Jean was saying inside her, not even her lips moving. *Come away, my wee Geordie.*

" I can't help it," the minister muttered. " I shouldn't be praying for a thing like that, but I canna' help it."

" . . . He heaved those great shoulders, flexed them once, a wonderful movement. And now he's in position. He's ready. He's all set. Any moment now. Bending for the spring. That kilt! He's off. Oh, the strength and the grace of the boy. Up it goes, up and up, and Geordie's safe inside the circle. It's coming down now. It's a beauty! My God, *he's won!* It's out clear in front of all the others. Oh, oh, oh. . . ." The far away American was speechless.

The minister jumped to his feet, knocking his chair over, face like a red apple wet from the tap, and he danced around his study in a wild caper. " Whoopee! " he shouted. " Whoopee! " Of all the things for a Presbyterian minister to shout.

Jean's heart was too full to notice anything strange in his behaviour. The tears of joy were running down her cheeks.

But the announcer had got his voice back. " It's pandemonium," he screamed. " It's colossal! It's an All-American wow. Geordie's smiling, coming back out of the circle. The crowd's gone mad! They're storming the arena, running for him from all directions. In twenty years I've never seen . . .

" And Helga Sorensen got there first! She's in his arms! They're kissing. It's splendid! It's a union of giants. It's beautiful to see. I wish you could see them, the kilted hero and the Nordic Diana. She's a lovely girl. What a couple! They're still embracing. The crowds are reaching him now."

Jean leaned forward quickly and turned off the switch. Then she stood up. The minister had stopped his capers. The smile was off his face.

" Perhaps . . ." he began. " Maybe . . ." But he looked greatly distressed.

Geordie came to his senses and disentangled himself from Helga. The first hand grasped his and spoke loud and foreign. " *Herzliche Glückwünsche!*" said Weber the mighty German, a bigger build of man even than Geordie.

" Thanks," said Geordie.

Then he was engulfed in the rampaging raving cheering crowd. They swung him up, all 20 stone of him, and he was tossed about precariously on their shoulders, smiling down at the laughing faces, at all the different kinds of faces with the stamp of America on them. Somewhere in among the confusion he heard the loudspeaker say " . . . Winner Geordie MacTaggart, Great Britain, 55 feet and half an inch. New Olympic Record." Louder cheering after that; noise and colour and heat and enthusiasm, and him surging round the grass of the arena. " Hi, Geordie! . . . Good work! . . . Great stuff, Geordie! . . . That was mighty fine! . . . That was wonderful! . . . How d'you like the States?"

"It's no bad," said Geordie. "It's nice for a visit. It's a fine place."

He was thoroughly happy in his strange position; but in a funny way, even as they took him round the track in triumph, even as he thought, "It's just as well I've the trews on underneath for decency's sake," even in the welter of bright noise and colour, Geordie's time with the kind Americans was over. He had started on his journey home.

They were just coming down the stretch beside the stands when he noticed a commotion within the commotion, a wedge forcing its way through the crowd below him, and stentorian voices shouting for passage; "Make way! Watch your hat, Lady! Gangway!" They were four or five large men in pale suits and pale hats, and being concerted in their action and determined, they forced their way through the jubilant crowd like a Sherman tank going through a field of corn. A chap in an army hat came trailing in their wake.

"Steady, folks!" he shouted. "Time to let Geordie go. Put him down gently. The President wants to meet him."

Geordie found himself back on the ground. The crowd stood close around him and the five big men and the military aide, for it was no less a person. The people were quiet now, smiles still on their faces, wondering how their newly-beloved Geordie would hit it off with the high brass.

" Come on, Geordie," said the military aide, a jolly fellow. " Come and meet the President."

" The President of *Amerriky*?" said Geordie. He knew he'd said that wrong, but an awful lot of things had happened in a short time and he didn't rightly know whether he was on his ankle or his elbow. " I'm no dressed right for to meet the President." He looked down with dismay at his dusty kilt and spiked shoes and vest crumpled now.

" Come on, Geordie," said the military aide again. " You look swell in that rig."

So the G-men formed a circle round Geordie, and they all bustled off towards the President's box, Geordie looking more like a prize Celtic slave being escorted to the Roman market than anything else.

He came into the box. His spikes were sticking through the carpet into the wooden boards, so walking wasn't free and easy.

" I'm delighted to meet you, Mr. MacTaggart," said the President formal but friendly, just like as if Geordie was a pal already. " That was a great performance."

" Thank you, sir," said Geordie, shaking hands. He felt a blush coming up all over him, but there wasn't anything he could do about it.

" I'd like you to meet my wife." So Geordie shook hands with Mrs. President too. Then there was a shuffling round of the Yankee quality in the box and he found himself sitting between them.

Out in the arena things had quietened down again and the Ladies Shot-Putting was in progress. It was funny to see the few of them out there, just like he'd been a few minutes ago. It was funny to see the thing the other way round.

But neither the President nor Geordie nor Mrs. President paid much attention to the Ladies Shot-Putting. They were too busy having a rare chat together.

" What's that kilt you're wearing, Geordie? " asked the President. He'd just called him Mr. MacTaggart the once.

" That's a Black Watch kilt," said Geordie. " It was my dad's as a matter of fact." And because the two of them seemed such decent folk he told them all about the kilt.

" And your mother is alive? " said Mrs. President. She was a comfortable-looking body. Maybe she felt happy talking to a simple laddie like Geordie. Maybe she liked that better than being with the high-ups.

" Ay, mum's fine, mam."

" Tell us about your home," said the President.

So Geordie told them all about home, about the hill and his job and the grouse-shooting starting soon and the Laird with his daft notions. He even told them about Jean.

Just then the announcer said: " Helga Sorensen, Norway, leads with . . ."

" You'd better not tell Jean about Helga," said the President of the United States. He had wrinkles all round the eyes and a rare twinkle in them. He had a twinkle like a man who's seen a lot to laugh and cry about.

Funnily enough that was just what Geordie was thinking. He was worrying that Jean might be vexed if she knew about him and Helga kissing out there in public. She might get the wrong notion of it altogether.

" That's right, sir," he said. " But I couldna' help myself. Helga's that keen."

The President threw his head back and went into gusts and gales of laughter. He laughed till he was fit to bust.

" Hush, dear," said Mrs. President. " You're making an exhibition of yourself." But she was laughing a bit too.

" Are you going back to Scotland soon? "

" The sooner the better," said Geordie.

" America's a braw place," he added hastily

when he saw them smile, " but . . . well, hame's hame."

" True enough," said the President.   Then he told Geordie about his own home; and how he was always thinking of it and wanting to go back; and how he'd been a right keen fisher when he was a laddie.

Geordie was feeling tired after what had happened to him that morning, so he was glad in the end when Mrs. President said:

" We mustn't keep Geordie too long, dear.   He could easily catch cold after all the excitement and not even a sweater on."

" Well, good-bye, Geordie," said the President. " It's been a real pleasure meeting you.   If Jean's difficult, just tell her Helga was that keen you couldn't help it."

" Good-bye, sir," said Geordie, thinking that over. " Mebbe she'll no believe me, though."

" She'll believe you in the end," said Mrs. President, looking at Geordie, knowing that no nice girl could help believing him in the end.

So Geordie bowed with dignity and respect and made his way out of the box.   There was a loud burst of cheers and clapping from the stand.

* 13 *

McCRIMMON'S bus stopped, and Geordie got down with his suitcase and the hat-box in his hands. " Cheerio, Geordie," said the driver. The bus rattled away towards Drumfechan village.

Well, here he was at last, home again, and the white cottage fifty yards away with mum's flowers growing on the end wall and the patch of lawn she must have cut herself for him to come back to a tidy place.

It was the same but not quite the same. The dappled leaves of holly, the glimpse of bare hill between beech tree and oak, a pigeon cooing somewhere in the wood, stopping as always in the middle of his song so that there was more coo-cooing to expect and no ending to the sleepy voice. They were the same things to see and hear; and the smell of rain was the smell he had known on a thousand other summer days.

It was home. It was the dead branch you should have cut down long ago, the moss doing no good to grey slates on the roof, the edges of the path untrimmed, the familiar irritating pleasure of jobs undone and new ones coming up that you would have to do. And all a little nearer to you than it was the day you went away.

Geordie had those feelings in a quick wave as he walked towards the house on a dull afternoon in the month of August.

" Mum! Are ye there, Mum? " he called at the door.

" Geordie! " She came running from the kitchen; a bit heavy-footed since she started putting on weight in earnest, but she could move fast. She held him at arm's length. " Let's take a look at ye. No change that I can see. The same wee Geordie grown big." She gave him another hug and led the way into the kitchen.

Geordie left the hat-box in the porch, not wanting awkward questions; but he took up his suitcase. There was the fine burning oatmeally smell of bannocks on the range.

" It's grand to be back," he said, looking round the kitchen. He could feel the places he had been and the things that had happened to him in the last month sliding away into a corner of his mind.

" So you won the prize," said mum. She had

her back to him over at the range.   Mum never
took much time away from what she was doing.

"Ay."

"I had the wireless turrned on," she said.   "But
I was ower excited.   I was wearing myself to a
shadow, so I had to shut it off afore the finish."

"Ye'd still be a guid-sized shadow," said
Geordie.

"Get away now, Geordie.   Yon's no the way to
speak to yer mum."   They both laughed.

"I'll get myself changed," said Geordie.   He
went upstairs to his room and put on old clothes.
That was another good feeling, to be wearing
patched things again.   It was like dressing up for
a Saturday night social.

When he came down mum had tea ready for him.
He could hardly wait to get away up to the gardens
to find Jean, but he didn't want to be hurting
mum's feelings, so he took his time and ate a bigger
tea than he was hungry for.

Afterwards she came to the door with him.   "I
hear tell Mistress Robertson's leaving the Bighoose.
Her old dad's ailing."

"Is that so?" said Geordie.

"The Laird was telling me," said mum, looking
at him with a meaning in her face he didn't under-

stand the reason for. " The Laird's needing new help in the kitchen."

Then she noticed the white box. " Yon's like a lady's hat-box."

" Ay," said Geordie. He wished he'd thought of hiding it in the bushes.

" Did ye bring me a hat all the way from Amerriky? That's a kindness, Geordie, I must say." She was laughing all over her face, a terrible tease was mum.

Geordie remembered the handbag he'd bought for her, so he ran upstairs to get it. It was a big leather one, useful for shopping.

" It's a braw bag," she said. " But here's me needing a new hat."

Geordie picked up the round box by its string and went off up the path before mum could say any more. " Thanks, Geordie," she called after him.

It wasn't raining yet, but it was a heavy afternoon, the kind of day that midges would be a pest about your ears and neck, and you would slap slap at them knowing it would do no good. With the slow day and him thicker in the head than usual on account of getting home again, Geordie was half-way to the garden before he tumbled to what mum could have been meaning about new help being needed in the

Bighoose. She could have meant that she was the one the Laird was after getting; perhaps that would explain the jokes about Jean's hat too. Perhaps mum and the Laird were thinking Geordie might be getting married.

"Yoo-hoo, George." There was only one person that could be. Geordie stopped, feeling vexed that he should be caught with the hat-box in his hand. He dropped it and looked round.

The Laird was sitting at the foot of a tree. He had his field-glasses round his neck, long legs stretched out in front. You quite often came on him like that, craning his neck back to see some bird and his big Adam's apple sticking out in his throat. Geordie went over.

"Welcome, George. Wassail! Glad to be back?"

"I am that," said Geordie. "How're you keeping, sir?"

"Pretty well, thank you. Just watching a Great Spotted Woodpecker. A touch of lumbago, nothing to speak of."

"It's the wet earth gives you that," said Geordie.

"Sit down on the wet earth, George, and tell me your adventures. But first tell me how it feels to be famous."

"There's no difference in it, not after the first

hum in yer heid." For a moment Geordie was back in that crowded arena, tilting and sprawling on the shoulders of the crowd, hearing the strange noise of people cheering him.

" Not after the first fine careless rapture," said the Laird, smiling. " Never been famous myself so I can't speak. Sounds good sense, though. Now tell me all about it."

So Geordie sat down beside the Laird and told his story, making it brief. When he reached the actual shot-putting, the Laird stopped him.

" I heard that on the wireless," he said.

" Did you, sir? " said Geordie, surprised that the Laird would find time in among all his wee jobs.

" Yes. Fellow did it splendidly. Curious language, of course. Tell me, George . . ." The Laird hesitated for words, tugging at his moustache like he was a bit uneasy. " Tell me, George. What about this Norwegian girl, Helga something or other, if it's not a rude question? "

" Helga? How did you hear that, sir? " A vague cloud of discomfort appeared on the horizon of Geordie's mind. If the Laird knew . . .

" Couldn't help hearing, my dear fellow. That announcer chap said you were embracing in the middle of the ring. Not only said it; he went on about it."

" It wasn't me started it," said Geordie, feeling like a small boy again. " It was Helga."

" Were you only a sleeping partner? " said the Laird. " Tut-tut," he muttered. " Didn't mean that. What I mean is, didn't you do a bit of embracing too? Feller certainly gave that impression."

" I s'pose I did, sir, in a manner of speaking, just for a wee minute. I couldn't help myself."

" Wouldn't have mentioned it, George. Only I happened to meet the minister a few days ago, and he said Jean was very much upset." The Laird coughed. " Can't blame her really. Public embrace and all that. Oh, listen to that hammer-headed bird! " The woodpecker drummed like a small machine-gun, on and off, a burst of noise in the quietness of the wood with no breeze stirring.

Geordie took a piece of twig and began to carve furrows in the soggy earth, not seeing the marks he was making. All his bright expectations had faded; all his tall castles were in ruins. Jean wasn't a lassie who'd forgive a thing like that; Jean wouldn't believe there were times when a chap would have to kiss in self-defence. She'd never understand the fever of that moment far away in America, that moment after the strength which was her giving had flooded out of him, and the people running from all directions and Helga first into his arms—soft delightful wicked Helga who meant nothing to him. He groaned out loud.

" Don't worry too much, George," said the Laird kindly. " Just thought you'd better be warned."

" I had that," said Geordie. He stared through the wood. It was a dank gloomy place, and the wet was soaking through the seat of his breeks. " What am I to do, sir? "

" Dunno," said the Laird. " Long time since my amatory experience." He frowned, giving the problem his whole attention, or as much attention as he was ever able to give any one problem before another idea crossed his mind. Finally he cleared his throat, and for once he spoke without it being like a telegram. " If I were you, George," he said, " I would make a manly apology to the lady. I would say you just kissed the first thing that came to hand in the heat of the moment. I would say it was a thing full of sound and fury, signifying nothing. In short I would say it wasn't your fault. But I wouldn't be too lame about the whole affair. After all, accidents are sure to happen, and human frailty knows no bounds. Then if there is any further hostility I should buss the lady."

" What's buss? " said Geordie, who was paying close attention.

M

" Embrace her.   Grasp her in your arms and say
you won't have any more damn' nonsense."

" Jean's got a terrible fierce temper," said
Geordie doubtfully.

" Yes I know," said the Laird.   " That's why
you need a bit of fire yourself."

Geordie stood up.   " Well, thanks, sir," he said.
" I'm much obliged."   He still wasn't sure if the
Laird had given him good advice, but he was so
depressed and worried that any solution was better
than trying to make up his own mind what to do.

The Laird walked over to the path with him.
" If you're looking for Jean," he said, " I saw her
at the trout hole an hour ago.   She was fishing dis-
consolately.   I say, what's this? "   He stood with
his legs wide apart, looking down at the hat-box.

" That's for Jean," said Geordie.   " I got it in
a hat shop in America."

" The devil you did," said the Laird, his insatiable
curiosity aroused.   " Let's have a look, George."

Geordie undid the string, removed the lid, laid
back the tissue paper and took out the hat.   He'd
forgotten what a beauty of a hat it was—green straw,
red feathers, white veil and the purple grapes all
the way round.

" My God! " said the Laird.

" Isn't that a braw hat? " said Geordie with

pride.   He held it up against the sombre colours of the wood.

"Braw!" said the Laird.   His face was twitching with admiration.   "It's stupendous.   That's a hat to tickle any woman's fancy."

"Jean could wear it to the kirk," said Geordie.

"Yes, indeed."

Geordie put it back in its box and tied the string neatly.   "I got it special," he said sadly, for the hat was only a small patch of blue sky amid heavy clouds.

"Well, good luck George," said the Laird.   "I hope it does the trick."

He watched Geordie's large light-footed figure for the distance the path ran straight.   "A truly ghastly hat," he muttered to himself.   "But you never know.   Love is blind.   Love is blind indeed."

Then the woodpecker drummed again nearby.

* 14 *

JEAN was still there. He could see her sitting
with the rod in her hands at the place between
the tumble of the big burn which gathered water
from five miles of hill, at the pool which was called
the Trout Hole, a deep place below the fast water
and above the fast water. He watched her back
for a minute, thinking of all the miles he had gone
and come, and no happiness now in the meeting.
Good-bye, Geordie, said Helga with her lip quivering.
You will forget and I shall remember. Sorry for
Helga. Sorry for himself. What a time to get her
in his mind again.

But he had to decide how to start with Jean.
Would he pretend he didn't know she knew?
Would he just go on as if nothing had happened?
No, not that, not with Jean. He'd never manage
to deceive her. Better let her know he knew there
was trouble, but let her be the first to speak of it.
The cowardly way? Och yes, cowardly.

He put down the hat-box in the high bracken and

went on towards Jean. She hadn't moved, slim graceful waist tied round with a bright girdle, swell of her hips on the rock. Geordie's heart leapt at the sight of her. He waited till he was close in below the rushing white water.

" Jean! " he called quite loud.

She jumped, point of the rod flicking up and down, and turned. There wasn't any expression on her face, no welcome, no anger, but it was going pale. The fresh colour was draining from it.

He stood beside her on the rock, remembering a jumble of things which happened before, or did they ever happen? Jean put her hand down flat. It looked like she would get up and changed her mind and didn't.

" Can I sit down? "

" I canna' stop ye."

Geordie sat down. The line hung into the dead part of the pool. He watched it. There wasn't a suspicion of a crease of moving water on the line.

" What's the bait? " he said after a long time with the midges pestering him.

" Wasp maggots." She nodded to the tin box beside her.

He looked at them. They were at the best stage, white still, but with the shape of the wasp, each one tucked away in its own place in the spongy comb.

" Did you catch any? "

" Does it look like it? " She said these things, but there wasn't anger in her voice, just a deadness and a dislike.

" D'you remember yon time we got ten in the one afternoon? " Perhaps if he went on speaking she might come round, she might thaw out in the end; but having to raise his voice above the splashing water made it more of an effort each time, made what he said sound hollow.

Jean grunted. She raised the rod and swung the line up the pool. The maggot sank, twisted, disappeared.

" So you won," she said flatly.

" Ay," said Geordie. " I managed to win." He thought: *It was you made me win*. But he couldn't say it then when she was sour at him, when her face was shut off so that he might have been miles away and nearer than he was now. *Come away, my wee Geordie*. He shifted restlessly on the hard rock, moved further from her.

" What's the next championship you'll be after winning? "

" That's the last," he said loudly. " I've done wi' all yon havers."

" Havers? " she said, turning to look at him for the first time, not able to hide her surprise.

" Ay, havers," said Geordie. " Exercises, balanced development, throwing a round ball. The
whole thing's . . . the whole thing's daft. What's
the use of being strong?" Now he'd said the
thing he'd been thinking for a long time underneath but never been sure of till the day in Boston.
Now he'd said it, and in a way getting it out was a
load off his mind, even in the middle of his troubles
with Jean. Only he wouldn't like Henry Samson
to hear him.

" There's uses in being strong," she said,
frowning.

" That's no what you said before," said Geordie,
coming right back at her. First she said exercises
were daft. Then when you said that yourself, she
changed her mind. Where could you be with the
contrary craters?

" Here, let's have the rod," he said, taking it
from her so quick she couldn't argue. He put two
new maggots on the hook. There was a place he
knew in the far corner. The pool was all deep,
seven or eight feet, but in that corner a rock jutted
out a foot below the surface, and often a trout would
lie under it, getting his feed in a hidden place,
nothing showing to an otter or a man except perhaps
a slow weaving of the tail for a moment and a flick
and back under cover.

It was a difficult place to put the weighted bait. You had to swing it just right into the fast water and let it move a foot and a half below the surface, no more, no less.

Geordie missed the first time. He tried again. This one looked better. It was in the right spot below the white foam. The maggot just showed in the water, coming now to the rock, out of sight beneath.

The line jinked sharply on the surface, and Geordie struck. " Got him! " he said, forgetting everything in that thrill, keeping a sure touch on his fish, letting the reel rasp out in a short run, recovering the spare at once. It was a good-sized trout; the silvery belly flickered down there in deep water, and the line slid tautly to the top of the pool and cut its furrow back. Geordie took it slowly, keeping a hold on the fish, letting it wear itself out. It was nearer the surface now, lunging in the slow curve of a tired fish well-hooked, head rising, coming out of the water, mouth gaping, one more convulsive wriggle.

Geordie pushed the rod back into Jean's hands, lay on his stomach on the rock and stretched down for the trout.

" Three-quarters," he said, killing it with the edge of his hand. The trout quivered on the flat rock, red spots shining, life not yet faded. " That's the way to get them." He smiled at Jean; you couldn't quarrel when you were catching fish.

" That's the way to get them! " She mimicked the way he spoke, and then said bitterly: " Aye showing off, aye doing it better than other folk, aye perfection—that's Geordie MacTaggart."

Geordie's worries came back to him with a rush. Now he'd made it worse, showing off to her how to take a trout in a pool she knew well. Jean knew about that rock too, but she'd been fishing to pass the time, making the motions of it and not caring.

" Och, Jean! " he said, more contrite than ever. But it was no good going on like this, getting the sharp edge of her resentment. This could go on forever, slide into a hard dull quarrel that couldn't be mended. He would have to bring it up about Helga.

" You heard it on the wireless? " said Geordie, taking the plunge.

" Ay."

What did the Laird say? Manly apology . . . Kissed the first thing that came to hand . . . signifying nothing.

" I couldn't help myself, Jean. It was just after I'd won. Helga took a jump at me, and before I knew it she was kissing me, before I knew it we was tied up there in public and all the folk running from round about. It was just like getting a kiss from the first thing that came to hand."

" The first thing to hand and you had no hand in it! " cried Jean, shouting loud above the endless rush of water. " Poor Geordie getting a hug from his grandma. Is that the way of it? "

Her eyes were flashing fire now and her cheeks were flushed. Well, anything was better than that cold shut-off deadness, and her so alive and hot-blooded.

" Listen! . . . She's in his arms. They're kissing. It's a union of giants. It's beautiful to see. They're still embracing. I wish you could see them! " Jean did a passable imitation of the excited American voice. Then she came back into her own. " I can see them right enough. I can see you after what you promised and Miss Helga what's-her-name cuddle cuddle cuddling afore the crowd."

Geordie groaned. " It was only afore the crowd," he said. " There was never any private places in it."

" Only afore the crowd! That's just it. That's worse. And the whole of the glen listening on the wireless having a good laugh at *me*. It isn't you. You're the great Geordie getting kisses, and daft women hungered for ye. It's me! " Jean stared down at the water, gripping the rock so her knuckles showed white.

" I'm sorry, Jean," said Geordie. " It was the heat of the minute and never signified nothing. You wouldn't be pleased if I'd been off in the woods and bushes with Helga, would ye? "

" I'm no caring," said Jean.

" I was thinking of you when I kissed her." It was true; he had been.

Jean sprang up and stamped her foot. " That's the last straw. That's the finish. And let me tell you, Geordie MacTaggart, I was *not* thinking of you when I was out with Tom Gillespie last week and didn't get home till two in the morning."

" Tom Gillespie! " said Geordie slowly, and the anger rose slowly in him, in the roots of his hair, and he got slowly to his feet. " Tom Gillespie! " That was the chap worked in the garage. That was the smarmy-headed one who'd been hanging about Jean for a long time. That was a wee man Geordie didn't like anyway—thought he was clever, standing with his toes off the pavement on Saturday night saying—" Here comes the Clydesdale Stallion," so Geordie could hear him yet not be sure.

" What was you doing with Tom Gillespie? " he said, glaring at her. The anger was red in him, and cold too and shivery, gripping him all over.

Why shouldn't she? But the unreasoning unaccustomed rage brushed that out of his mind. Too much he'd taken from Jean Donaldson!

He towered over Jean beside the pool, but she was not afraid. She stared him back hotly in the eyes. " Why wouldn't I go with Tom Gillespie? Why wouldn't I get a kiss? "

Buss her! he thought blindly. That's what the Laird said. By God, he'd give her a bussing and a skelp she'd remember on her soft bottom. He'd pay her back for saying he hadn't been true.

Love, anger, jealousy, even a moment of hate were all mixed up in Geordie's seething mind. He lunged for Jean, gripped her by the shoulders, bent down to kiss her fiercely, but she fought like a wild cat, turning her head this way and that, teeth bared to get at his wrists. She's strong, he thought, watching her contorted fiery passionate beautiful face, seeing it for a bright second in his own anger, forcing her close to him now. But she twisted to right and left, back to right again, foot on the edge of the rock, a warm wonderful hateful lassie in his arms.

He got his lips against her cheek, and then he couldn't see and slipped and it was too late. They were still struggling as they hit the water, and the cold of the hill burn smacked him painfully on the head. They came apart gasping. Geordie's own anger died at once, but not Jean's. She attacked him in the water, tugging at his hair like a wet fury. But it was too difficult to keep up a fight in deep water, and Jean hardly able to swim, he knew that. In a minute she was clutching at him for safety.

Geordie held her head up and kicked for the side. It was a hard place to get out of. He remembered that from once when he'd fallen in as a laddie. The rocks dropped two feet sheer into the water.

" Hang on, Jeannie," he gasped, putting her hand to a small crevice. Then he found a hand-hold for himself, and another, inching himself up the rock with his great strength, getting both hands on top, drawing his body over the edge in a long heave.

He knelt and looked down at her. She was still spluttering, black hair in her eyes and floating out behind. She looked very much bedraggled, but her face was wet and bare and bonny.

" Are ye sorry, my wee Jean? " he said, all the resentment and rage wiped out of him, laughing at the fine pickle they'd got themselves into.

" No, I'm not," she panted.

" I'll leave ye then," said Geordie. Now at last he had her where he wanted to have her. " I'll leave ye till the trout nibble at your bones. I'll leave ye till the big spate comes and slides you higgle-piggle to the river and away out floating. Are ye sorry?"

"No," said Jean, but there was just a glimmer of a smile on her face with teeth chattering.

He bent far down for her wrists and lifted her right out in one movement, and she was in his arms now, both of them cold and wet, and no more thought of anger. They kissed one another till the heat of their two bodies joined through wet clothes, and there was a living warmth between them but backs still cold, so a reason to cling more tightly, feeling the sharp sweetness of love after anger, of meeting after absence.

"I never let Tom Gillespie kiss me," Jean murmured.

Geordie said nothing, wise in his generation, wise in the wisdom of that daft old Laird. Buss her and no more damn' nonsense. No more explaining from him.

"We'll need to get changed, Geordie, Geordie darling," said Jean into his ear. She'd never called him that before. Such a word as Darling would not come easily to them. She drew back from him, but not turning away, not shy to have him watch the wet dress lie close to the lines of her body, not shy to be there for him to see.

" Am I better than Helga? "

Geordie laughed out loud. He felt he could laugh forever. And well he might, for that is the magic moment in a man's life. It comes but once, although you might imagine you discovered it again.

He took her to him. " Ay, you're better'n Helga—better this way and that way, better every way. Stronger and fiercer and less muscles on ye, and you're the one I'm loving." Just the shadow of Helga, the faint discomfort of taking from a woman what you could not give; the thing that never does quite leave you; but you pay no heed to it.

" I've a hat for ye, Jean."

" A hat? "

" Ay. I looked at every hat in the window in Boston and chose it special. You could wear it to the kirk. You could wear it on the Marriage day."

" Oh, Geordie! Let's see."

He picked up the rod, fixed the bare hook into the handle, took the trout by the gills, and walked with Jean to the bracken where the hat-box lay. It was a queer place to leave a hat from Boston. That was a feeling Geordie had.

The clouds were still lower now, and it had begun

to drizzle, but they were too happy and wet already and shivering for that to make a difference.

Jean knelt to undo the string, fumbling in her eagerness.

" Oh! " she said, holding it up in the rain. " Oh! "

Then she burst into tears. Well, of all the things for Jean to do just then, just when she had the hat in her hand at last.

" Do ye no think yon's a braw hat? " said Geordie. A terrible thought had struck him.

" My wee Geordie," she sobbed, coming to him; so with hat and trout and rod there was just the one hand to spare between the two of them. " And you bringing it all the way from America. It's the . . . It's the bonniest hat I ever saw."

" Put it on," he said.

Jean flung back her wet hair and put the braw hat on her head.

The drizzle thickened, making a tiny shaking patter on the leaves. The mist was cold and close about them as they went home. But Geordie and Jean could see the rolling of the hill. They knew the moods which gave it life. They saw the sweep of it with no ending.

THE END